HOLD ON, LET GO

not beyond repair

Nicole Rothell

Originally published in the United States by N.T.R. Publishing

ISBN 10: 0999621602
ISBN 13: 9780999621608
Library of Congress Control Number: 2017917414
N.T.R Publishing, Richmond, TX

ACKNOWLEDGMENTS

A huge thanks to my father, who always
nurtured my imagination.

CHAPTER ONE

The world outside moved faster and faster as the old, outdated 1970s Chevrolet truck traveled down the highway. The crimson paint reflected the rising sun, creating a bright sheen on the hood. Oliver Murray squinted at the sudden glare of sunlight, and after a moment of thought, a subtle expression of annoyance flickered across his face. Blinking his eyes against the rays, he repositioned himself in the passenger seat and stared solemnly out the grimy window. It was weird how quickly the trees and cars were whipping by, almost like a movie stuck in fast-forward. All of it felt so surreal. Simply unrealistic.

The sixteen-year-old boy shifted again in the seat. With a discreet little sigh, he moved to get a better view out the window. Slowly, the dense number of houses and buildings reduced to a few small farmhouses that lined the outskirts of the city. Eventually the trappings of civilization vanished as the scene melted away into a vast forest that spread over the gently rolling hills of the countryside. Suddenly, the wall of trees stopped at a clearing, and a large lake came into sight. Early-morning sunlight danced across the shimmering blue waters of the lake from one end to the other.

Oliver gazed at the scenery in awe. It had been a while since he had seen the country. All this time he had been trapped in the city with nowhere to go. In fact, it had been almost five months since the accident. He shuddered, trying to push the awful memory that haunted him every day to the very back of his mind. But he couldn't forget due to a painful reminder that plagued his life: muffled noises. The unpleasant fact was that now hearing was an everyday struggle that he would battle for the rest of his life. The void of various sounds rang in his ears day after day; at first their absence was so hideous that it was almost unbearable.

How could it get worse? he pondered silently. First the accident, the loss, and the hospital, and then going through foster care, and now an uncle he had never met before was taking him to meet some farm family who were supposedly his relatives. Turns out he had met them once when he was very young, but he didn't know them any better than he did his uncle. Oliver glanced over at his uncle, who was sitting in the driver's seat and talking on his cell phone, despite it being illegal to make calls and drive at the same time. He didn't even know his uncle's name yet. Just calling him plain old Uncle Nameless would have to do for now.

To shake off the bad memories, Oliver tried to focus his mind somewhere else. Gazing at the scenery was not helping. Well, maybe a little, but not much. With nothing else to do, Oliver just set his attention on studying the stranger who was his so-called uncle. Slowly, he took in the details: His uncle had graying black hair that was receding from the front of his head. A thin gray mustache lined his upper lip, and his face was somewhat long and narrow but rounded like an oval. Creases formed under his hazel eyes, showing off his age, while he squinted against the bright glare of the sunlight and talked on the phone.

Oliver could not help but feel slightly amused as he watched his uncle pin the phone on his shoulder and hold the steering wheel while he attempted to open the lid on a flimsy foam cup of coffee. Uncle Nameless scraped at the lid, which was stuck firmly on the shoddy cup. It was amazing how cheap some fast-food restaurants could be. How did they expect to safely serve hot coffee in paper-thin cups made out of foam?

It's utterly ridiculous, Oliver thought in disgust as he watched his uncle fumble with the mess. The cup threatened to split open each time his uncle tried to peel off the lid. With a wary eye kept on the cup, Oliver scooted farther away from the accident that was about to happen. He had a bad feeling about this.

Peeved by the situation, Uncle Nameless talked faster on the phone and started to rip at the stubborn lid. Suddenly, the whole seam on the side of the cup burst. Steaming-hot coffee spilled out into a lava flow across his lap. The truck swerved on the road, and he let out a spurt of cuss words as he grabbed the steering wheel. Oliver held on for dear life.

Still fuming over the incident, Uncle Nameless quickly pulled over on the side of the road and parked. His face turned red as a beet while he picked his coffee-soaked phone up off the floorboard. Muttering, he hastily grabbed the now-empty cup, rolled down the window, and tossed it out. Obviously he did not care about the littering laws. Uncle Nameless rolled the window back up and then finished the conversation on his cell phone, all the while curling his lip up into a snarl as he stared down at his coffee-soaked jeans.

Oliver had to turn away and stare out the window to keep from laughing. He would surely get a good scolding about lack of respect for his uncle if he started to laugh. He tried and tried to suppress the snicker that tickled at his lips, aching to come out. Somehow he managed to keep a straight face. Finally, after what seemed like hours, they got on the road again, heading for their destination. It was going to be a long drive; they had to travel out of South Carolina and reach Virginia, where his relatives lived. Oliver sighed and slouched in his seat.

Might as well sit back and enjoy the ride.

CHAPTER TWO

Jennifer Murray stood by and watched as her restless grandmother paced back and forth by the front door, stopping every once in a while to peek outside through the freshly cleaned windows. They had been waiting for the arrival of her uncle, who was late. Jennifer didn't understand what the big deal was. It wasn't like it was that urgent for her uncle to arrive early. In fact, she didn't mind at all that he had not arrived yet. The later the better, in her opinion.

The suspense of waiting was a mixture of excitement and dread all at the same time. Jennifer did enjoy seeing her uncle from time to time, but this visit was different; tonight she would see her estranged cousin for the first time in years. Even worse, he would be moving in with them. She had always been an only child, taken care of by her grandparents since she was three. After her grandfather had passed a while ago, it was just her and Granny. Jennifer kind of liked it that way too, because she got all the undivided attention. But pretty soon, everything would change. She didn't feel ready at all to meet her cousin. She most definitely wasn't prepared to share her life with someone other than Granny.

"What do you think he'll be like?" Jennifer eventually asked.

Temporarily distracted from her worrying, Granny stopped pacing. Jennifer watched Granny's anxiety transmit to her twiddling thumbs, which churned like a perpetual watermill, circulating a stream of emotions. Through all the chaos of cleaning the house and getting things ready, she had failed to tend to her own appearance, which was unlike Granny. Her short curly hair, splotched and faded by age, was a real mess. She had even forgotten to take off her apron after cooking a last-minute dinner that afternoon.

"If you're referring to your cousin, I'm not really sure."

Unsatisfied with the vague answer she got, Jennifer mulled over the dozens of questions she had. In reality, she knew nothing about her cousin other than the fact that he had been involved in an unfortunate accident that had left him without his family.

"Don't worry about it," Granny tried to reassure her. "Just be your normal self and be friendly."

Easier said than done. Jennifer couldn't help but roll her eyes at Granny, who had resumed fluttering around nervously. It was hard to be calm and unworried when someone else was close to having a panic attack.

Tall trees lined the sides of the lonely road. Branches covered in thick green leaves towered above, creating a shadowy canopy. The gravel from the road flicked on the sides of the truck as it slowly meandered along the mazelike road. It was now dusk, and the sun was slowly creeping out of sight behind the partially hidden horizon. The orange rays of light flickered through the wall of trees like fingers of fire. Darkness had cast an eerie look on the quiet road, and shadows were everywhere, ready to trick the tired eyes of the driver and passenger in the old battered truck.

Oliver shifted in the seat for the hundredth time. He was tired of being in the vehicle. An irritating cramp in his neck was bugging him, determined to make him go mad. He wiggled again in the seat. This time he got a harsh look from his uncle. Oliver immediately stopped moving and sat quietly.

Hey, I can't help it, he thought in annoyance. *Never asked to come on this crazy trip anyway.*

With a big sigh, he returned to looking out the window. Suddenly another cramp flared up. Oliver winced but did his best to ignore it. It started to hurt worse, so he slowly sat up straighter. So far his uncle paid no attention to his fidgeting. He could feel the devious cramp just inching its way up his side and around his shoulder. *Ouch!* he thought as he rubbed his shoulder with his hand. Oliver glanced over at his uncle, who was still staring off into space. Taking the opportunity, he wiggled his shoulder, trying desperately to get the cramp out.

He was so focused on his aching shoulder that he never noticed that they were pulling into the driveway. Realizing that the vehicle had come to a halt, he looked up in surprise. They had finally arrived!

Bathed in the dark evening light, a big yellow farmhouse with white trim loomed in front of them. The white railing marked the perimeters of the ancient porch. The window shutters were also white and old fashioned. For a last touch, a lonely wooden rocking chair sat on the porch. Its only company was its own shadow, which stretched across the front of the house. Basically everything about the house was outdated and weird. It resembled a haunted Halloween house in a horror movie. The only additional things it needed were a creepy black cat to saunter around and maybe a cackling witch or even a werewolf. But then again, the house was already freaky enough on its own.

Uncle Nameless wasted no time in jumping out of the truck and grabbing Oliver's small suitcase out of the back. Oliver hesitated before getting out himself. What would it be like? Here he was, about to meet his new family. For a moment, he had the insane thought of just locking the doors of the pickup truck and refusing to get out. His hand brushed the lock button on the door.

Should I? he asked himself. He quickly abandoned the idea when he noticed that his uncle was standing on the porch and looking at him with a cold, hard stare. It almost looked like a replay of Stonewall Jackson or something. Somehow it seemed that Uncle Nameless knew what he was thinking.

Maybe I shouldn't. Still fretting, Oliver slowly got out of the truck and took a few stiff steps toward the house, where his uncle awaited him. It was good to stretch out his long legs; they felt like knotted-up Slinkies. Each step was agonizing as he made his way up the wooden porch steps. He reached his uncle and stood next to him. Uncle Nameless impatiently jabbed repeatedly at the doorbell with his boney finger, as if he was in no mood to wait. They both stood for about five minutes, staring at the weathered door. White paint was flaking off in some spots. The bottom of the door was completely stripped of paint. All too soon, in Oliver's opinion, the door opened.

A woman who was probably in her seventies stood in the doorway. Streaks of gray showed in her faded red hair, which was a wildfire of untamed curls. She had an apron on too, with pastel-pink and baby-blue flowers dancing across it. It looked worse than a piece of old-timey wallpaper. A dainty little pair of spectacles rested on her nose, making her look bug eyed.

Is this my grandmother? Oliver thought anxiously.

With a big smile stretched from ear to ear, his supposed grandmother greeted them and welcomed them inside. Oliver trailed closely behind his uncle as they went in. After having them sit down in the living room, the old woman fluttered about and went to get drinks for everyone.

Looking around, Oliver realized that the inside of the house was in much better shape than the outside. Although it still had a strange taste of decor—the couches were a sunny yellow and made out of a velvety material, and a big carpet rested on the polished hardwood floor, radiating in colors of white, green, yellow, and blue. The colors resembled two things: when he looked at the carpet straight on, he could see the colors of bluebell flowers and yellow daisies in a big prairie field, or when he eyed the carpet from an angle, he saw a disgusting pile of vomit. It was all up to the person to decide what it looked more like. Oliver settled on imagining it as a prairie of flowers. There would not be anything less pleasant than imagining walking on a field of vomit every day. The coffee table was a mahogany brown. A big vase of fresh flowers had been placed in the middle of it. Of course, the flowers were the same wonderful colors as the carpet.

The end tables were also a mahogany brown to match the coffee table. A few pictures hung on the walls as well. Two of them were apparently portrait paintings: One was of a young woman, who looked quite like a younger version of Oliver's grandmother. The other was of some man, perhaps her husband. Oliver looked about the room again and lastly noticed an ancient television sitting in the corner facing the couch.

At least they're civilized enough to have TV here, Oliver thought. *I hope they have Internet, too.*

Oliver shifted uncomfortably on the couch when he saw the old lady emerge into the living room again, holding a tray with two cups of tea. A can of Coke was on the tray as well, clashing with the antique theme of the frilly tea set. The lady beamed a big smile at Oliver and handed him the Coke. He eagerly took it, thankful to have something to drink after being stuck in the rickety truck for ages. It had been nothing other than utter torture.

CHAPTER THREE

T he staircase couldn't have been a better hiding spot. Hidden from view, Jennifer was able to peer through the railing without being noticed. She wasn't a shy person, but she couldn't find the courage to go downstairs and introduce herself. It was just unnerving, seeing Oliver after all those years.

When she had first gotten the news about her cousin moving in, Jennifer had the brilliant idea to open her ancient laptop and look him up on Facebook to learn a little about him before he arrived. With a bit of re-searching, she figured out that her cousin was a year older than she was, had a passion for music, and used be on a school track team. There wasn't much indication of his personality though, therefore making it difficult to judge what he was really like in person. From what Jennifer could remember after having met him once when his family had come over for a visit, Oliver was lighthearted and playful. He had also been a bossy little kid, which caused him and Jennifer to clash. They had both wanted everything *their* way, and they had been unwilling to compromise, since they were equally stubborn. That fact alone had made the previous visit less than pleasurable.

I wonder if he's still just as hardheaded.

Jennifer pressed herself against the railing to get a better look at the three people in the living room. Her uncle was sitting on the couch, discussing things with Granny. Slouched next to him was Oliver, seemingly detached from the world as he stared off into the distance. He remained eerily still, as if he were frozen in place and unaware of the conversation that was taking place. His grim face was so rigid and tense it could have been a windswept gravestone. The only signs of life were his penetratingly pale eyes, which were darting from side to side as if he were taking note of everything in his new surroundings. His shaggy blond hair was unruly, as if he hadn't touched it in days.

His look made Jennifer think of a caged wolf she had seen at a zoo when she was little. She could remember the same expression of distrust on its face as it had stared warily into the crowd of onlookers.

⊶⊷

Although he was in the same room with them, Oliver heard nothing but muffled sounds as Uncle Nameless spoke with the old woman. Wishing he could hear what they were saying, Oliver stared solemnly at the empty can of Coke he held in his hands. The white words that spelled *Coca-Cola* on the side contrasted against the bright-red metal. The perky colors were dull to him though. His mind was elsewhere. He wanted to know what was being said, to know what plans were in store for him. Living in an almost soundless world was becoming normal for him, but the familiar feeling of frustration soon began to envelop him as he tried to listen.

Finally giving up trying to follow the conversation, Oliver turned his attention to the unfamiliar surroundings again. As he scanned the living room, he paused when he spotted movement. Turning his head, he looked toward the old wooden stairs. Behind the recently polished wooden railing sat a figure, crouched as if not wanting to be seen. A pair of green eyes peered at him with burning curiosity. The intense stare sent a shiver down his spine. Oliver flinched.

Well, that's creepy, he thought as he gazed back at the figure.

Suddenly, as if realizing Oliver had spotted it, the figure quickly stood halfway, revealing that it was actually a girl. She scurried back up the stairs as fast as she could. A flash of red hair whipped behind her as she bolted up the steps. The sudden commotion disturbed the conversation, bringing it to a halt. Oliver glanced over at his grandmother and uncle, hoping for an explanation. He got none though. Instead, his grandmother placed her cup of tea on the coffee table and stood. She said something to Uncle Nameless and excused herself before heading upstairs. It didn't take long for her to come back with the same redheaded girl who had been spying on them. Oliver's breath caught in his throat. He remembered her all too well—the smart-alecky girl who thought she knew everything. How could he ever forget?

Just my luck, I wind up having to live with my least favorite cousin.

Jennifer looked a lot different from the last time he had seen her; she was no longer a stumpy toddler waddling about but was now a fifteen-year-old with a lot of energy. Even though they were cousins, they did not look very much alike. She was petite and lithe, unlike Oliver, who was tall and slightly awkward. Bright flaming hair fell just below her shoulders and framed her oval face, the one feature that seemed to run in the family. Her eyes were a brilliant green, like two glittering emeralds. A few freckles danced across her sun-kissed skin, and her dainty lips were perverted into a mischievous smirk, as if she had a ton of things to say. Apparently she wasn't ashamed of having been caught snooping around.

However, Jennifer's haughty smile quickly vanished when her grandmother said that she needed to show Oliver to his new room. Reluctantly, she followed instructions and did as she was told.

"Fine." Her voice was somewhat audible as she waved Oliver over. "C'mon; follow me upstairs." He could just barely make out the country accent in her drawling voice, yet another thing that differed between them as cousins.

Without saying a word, Oliver got up and trailed behind Jennifer, letting her lead him to the bedroom that had been prepared for him. As he walked in, he let his gaze skim over the neatly swept room. The first thing he noticed was a ready-made bed, which he so longed to crash in. The navy-blue bedcover was tucked in nicely, with three pillows neatly placed at the headboard. One of them, a black throw pillow, stood out from the other pillows. Embroidered on it was a light-blue horse head. Oliver looked at the bed for a moment longer before taking in the rest of the details of the room. Framed pictures of horses hung on the beige walls.

One in particular that was hanging above the headboard of the bed was familiar; the picture portrayed a large brown-and-white paint horse, posed for the camera. On the horse's back was a small boy with a smile that went from ear to ear. At the horse's head was a tall man with medium-brown hair and a neatly trimmed beard. He held onto the horse's bridle while smiling at the camera. The picture gave Oliver an immediate flashback. The little boy was him when he was five years old, and the man was his father. Another old memory.

Not wanting to look at the picture any longer, he turned away and focused his attention on Jennifer, who was standing by the door with her arms crossed. She tapped her foot in an unsubtle way, signifying that she was getting impatient. It was easy to tell that she didn't exactly appreciate Oliver's intrusion into her life, and she wasn't going to bother making the effort to be overly welcoming.

Yeah, I'm happy to see you too, Oliver thought sarcastically.

Suddenly the bedroom door opened, putting an end to the uncomfortable apprehension between them. They looked up as the uninvited guest stepped into the room. It was Uncle Nameless, coming in to say goodbye. A feeling of sadness swept over Oliver. He didn't want to see his uncle leave. He didn't want to say goodbye to the last person who he sort of knew, and he most certainly did not want to be left behind in this country farmhouse with these strangers. He didn't want to be here in Virginia. He just wanted desperately to go back home.

But that just isn't going to happen, he told himself as his uncle awkwardly gave him a hug, a pat on the head, and a quiet few words of encouragement, or whatever it was he said. Then Uncle Nameless left the room as silently as he had arrived a few moments earlier. With a feeling of helplessness, Oliver glanced at Jennifer. The scrutinizing glare she had was starting to become unnerving. To his relief, her scowl finally softened a little.

"OK then," she said crisply. "I'm heading out. I guess I'll let you get settled into your room. Goodnight." With that, Jennifer spun on her heel and left, leaving Oliver all alone.

Even with a hearing loss, it wasn't hard to catch that tone. Oliver mulled over what had happened that day and sighed. He was too tired to even think. *Jeez, it'll be a miracle if I can crawl into that bed.* After absentmindedly pulling off his tennis shoes and socks, Oliver trudged over to the bed and warily climbed in. With a big yawn, he flopped his head back on the soft, cushy pillow and let out a breath of relief as he quickly drifted off to sleep.

CHAPTER FOUR

I t was the sun coming in through the window that woke Oliver. He sat up in the bed and yawned. *Where am I? How'd I get here?* he wondered. Then his eyes popped all the way open as he looked around the unfamiliar bedroom. Slowly, he slipped out from underneath the navy-blue comforter and stumbled around as he suddenly remembered where he was.

Oh man, what a day that was, he thought, recalling yesterday's events.

Now more awake, Oliver glanced toward the wooden bedroom door, wondering whether he should get dressed and go downstairs. But he chickened out, not wanting to deal with adjusting to his new family just yet. Curious about what it looked like outside, he stepped up to the bedroom window and drew the curtains back. Once he recovered from being temporarily blinded by the bright light that spilled into the room, he stared out the window in awe as he took in the details of the magnificent view.

In the distance was a modest-size wooden barn cloaked in traditional red, its stark white accents glinting under the sun. Flower bushes were planted around the barn's entrance, adding small bursts of color. A meandering gravel path led from the barn all the way to a riding arena close by. In the arena, a few show jumps were set up, ready for use. On the other side of the barn was a large fenced-in pasture, which was occupied by two horses that were contentedly grazing in the lush sea of green. The spectacle was so perfect that it looked like a painting of some dreamlike wonderland.

Oliver grinned. This place definitely wasn't a farm with cows, chickens, and pigs. It was actually a horse stable right behind the house. *Wow. Simply wow,* he thought in amazement. It seemed almost too good to be true, but it was *there* and as real as the barricading glass that stood between him and the whimsical scenery.

⊶⊷

"Typical city kid—lazy," Jennifer stated through a mouthful of scrambled eggs. "I can't believe he's sleeping in so late. It's already six forty!"

Granny shook her head at the inconsiderate comment as she fixed herself a bowl of special organic cereal filled with various nuts and berries. The milk was organic too. It was what she dutifully ate every single morning. Jennifer never understood why her grandmother wouldn't eat something more appetizing, like bacon for example, or normal cereal at least. Even though Granny insisted that it was healthy and nutritious, Jennifer still didn't believe her. She felt that her grandmother's obsession with healthy food was all a bunch of baloney.

After spooning some honey out of a jar into her bowl of cereal, Granny sat down at the kitchen table. "Oliver's had a rough time; give him a break. However, I must say I'm still surprised he didn't want to come down for dinner last night."

"Um…I forgot to ask," Jennifer admitted. She winced when Granny gave her an appalled look. Trying to avoid getting in trouble, she quickly made up an excuse, which was partially true. "I didn't think he'd understand me anyway, since he's deaf."

"He is not completely deaf," Granny corrected. "He can still hear a little; all you have to do is speak up loudly for him."

"Oh, does that mean he's not mute either?"

"Now what on earth would make you think that he can't speak?"

"I don't know; I just thought…well, never mind."

"I swear, you get some of the funniest notions sometimes. It's getting late. I suggest that you go up and check on him. See if he wants anything for breakfast."

Working hard to hide her annoyance, Jennifer got up from the table and headed upstairs. She didn't appreciate that she had somehow been given the responsibility to look after her cousin. Why did she have to deal with him? It was bad enough having to accept that he was going live with her and Granny. What a horrible nightmare. How could it be true?

Once she arrived at the spare bedroom, which was now assigned to Oliver, Jennifer knocked on the door. No answer. She knocked again and waited. Still no response. Feeling irritated, she raised her hand to bang on the door but then caught herself.

Duh, he can't hear! Jennifer bit her lip in exasperation while she turned the brass knob and let herself in. There were definitely going to be a lot of things to get accustomed to, like this for instance.

Startled by her unexpected entry, Oliver sat up abruptly on the bed and stared. To Jennifer's surprise, he wasn't asleep after all. In fact, he had been playing with his iPod and even had a little bit of music on.

What in the world is he doing with an iPod? Jennifer wondered before saying, "Breakfast's ready. Wanna come down?"

Oliver answered by shaking his head no. For whatever reason, he just wasn't saying much.

"Aren't you hungry?"

Another head shake confirmed that he was not.

"OK, suit yourself." Giving up on trying to persuade him to come downstairs, Jennifer left her speechless cousin alone. She had better things to do than trying to carry on a pointless conversation.

If he doesn't want to talk, so be it. Maybe it's a good thing! I won't have to worry about arguing with him like last time.

It was a pleasurable sensation when Jennifer lifted the English saddle off of the rack. Upon touching the smooth chocolate-colored leather, which was supple from regular conditioning, a tingle of excitement ran from the tips of her fingers up her arms like electricity. It was purely the anticipation of getting ready to ride that gave her the rush of adrenaline. The temporary high of forgetting everyday issues and focusing entirely on being aboard a horse—a regal animal so full of power and grace. Although horses could be dangerous, the love and delicate bond of trust they offered compensated for the risks involved with riding them.

Cradling the saddle in her arms, Jennifer meandered down the barn aisle. The large dappled-gray gelding that stood tethered by the crossties shifted and eyed her as she came up. The horse flicked an ear toward her and nickered softly, likely wondering whether any treats were coming his way.

"Sorry, Pompeii, you'll have to wait."

The horse dropped his head disappointedly and blew air through his nostrils like a dragon, reminding Jennifer just how volcanic he was. Pompeii had earned his name for a reason: he was as explosive as dynamite and ready to detonate if anything ever sparked around him. Even though Jennifer had owned him for over two years, he was still just as difficult to handle as he had been in the beginning. They had managed to successfully win first place in only one show out of about five. This was a hideous burr under Jennifer's saddle. She had hoped that retiring her old horse and starting over with a new one would help catapult her into the next level of show jumping. So far it wasn't really happening.

Soon enough, Jennifer had her horse tacked up. Once she made sure all the gear was secure and in place, she led Pompeii out to the arena. She then halted him, lifted her left foot into the stirrup, and with one sweeping motion, swung herself into the saddle. Feeling the weight on his back, Pompeii shifted and stretched around with his head, reaching toward Jennifer's leg. When she didn't notice and continued to straighten her riding gloves, the horse swished his tail in annoyance and bit at the end of her boot—not hard but enough to leave an unsightly scuff mark on the toe.

Yanking her foot away from the ornery horse's mouth, Jennifer scowled. *Great, I hope I can smooth out that scratch. Dumb horse. What did you do that for?*

Glancing at Pompeii's unsympathetic face, Jennifer realized she had forgotten to give him a treat after he had waited obediently. Because Pompeii didn't use to stand still long enough for her to mount, she had created a routine where she always rewarded him whenever he stayed put after she got on.

"Oops, almost forgot." Jennifer reached into the pocket of her riding breeches. Eager for his treat, Pompeii stretched his head around again. The metal snaffle bit jangled noisily as he opened his mouth. Not wanting to get another dent in her boot, Jennifer hurriedly leaned over and shoved a sugar cube between the horse's groping lips.

Pompeii inhaled the sugar cube and demolished it with a gnash of his teeth. Now satisfied, he let out another one of his dragon snorts and trundled forward in an energized, sweeping walk.

CHAPTER FIVE

The sensation of gnawing hunger finally lured Oliver out of the bedroom. After not having eaten the previous day or that morning, by dinnertime his stomach felt as if it were being turned inside out—not a fun thing to experience.

I wouldn't survive being stranded on an island, Oliver thought miserably as he stood at the top of the stairs, which in his mind seemed more ominous than gazing into the black never-ending abyss of a cave entrance. He battled with himself, trying to decide whether or not to get dinner. Unable to ignore the rumbling in the empty cavern of his stomach, he swallowed his fear and made himself walk down the stairs, putting one foot in front of the other. The old wooden steps creaked underneath his shoes, but he didn't notice.

Oliver ventured into the living room, wondering which way the kitchen was. *Where is everybody?* No one was in the living room, although the TV had been left on, testifying that there was some form of life inside this seemingly vacant house. After absentmindedly walking a full circle around the entire living room, he exited and headed down the hallway. As he got to the end, he smelled something. *Food.* Inhaling the delicious, mouthwatering scent, Oliver followed it to the kitchen. He tried to make out the individual scents, hoping to know what was cooking. From what he could figure out, it was a combination of cheese, marinara sauce, and something else that he had not yet identified—maybe a hint of garlic. It was hard to tell.

As he stood at the kitchen's entrance, absorbing the appealing odors, he soon had the sense of being watched. Whirling around, he spotted two faces staring intently at him from the dining room, which was parallel to the kitchen area. On the wooden surface of the aged dinner table was a large box of delivered pizza, obviously the source of what Oliver had smelled earlier.

Realizing that he had not said one word to Jennifer and their grandmother since he had arrived, Oliver started to feel awkward and a bit embarrassed at himself. He never intended to be rude, but he felt self-conscious about trying to communicate now that he had trouble hearing. Even his own voice sounded kind of muted to him.

What do I say to them? Not knowing what else to do, he gave a small halfhearted wave and said, "Hey."

"Hey?" That's all you could think of to say after we haven't talked to one another in years? Unbelievable.

Jennifer kept her thoughts to herself and bit into a slice of pizza, savoring the warm melted cheese. The pepperoni was just right too, slightly crunchy with a hint of spice. She didn't think much of the olives and mushrooms though, which Granny had ordered in an attempt to "healthify" the pizza. As if they would make much difference.

"Would you like to sit down?" Granny asked when Oliver remained where he was, as if his feet were glued to the floor.

Breaking out of his trance, Oliver nodded and un-planted himself. For the first time, Jennifer noticed that he walked with a faint limp when he came to the table and sat down next to her. He relaxed some-what but still had that anxious vibe. If a person could sink in a lake of nerves, they'd all be drowning by now. Oblivious to the thick tension floating around the room, Granny snagged a plate and served a slice of pizza to Oliver, who didn't hesitate to dig in. He must've been starving, judging from the way he ate: shredding his food apart like an animal, he gobbled it down ravenously. For a city kid, he didn't have the greatest of manners. It made Jennifer look refined for once.

Granny and Jennifer exchanged glances, both feeling sympathy for Oliver. Neither of them knew exactly what he had been through; they had received limited information about the accident. It was clear though that it was going take a while for him to adjust.

"So, how was the trip out here with your uncle?" Granny attempted to strike up a conversation. It wasn't really her style, eating in silence.

Jennifer paid close attention, wondering what her voiceless cousin would say. Since Granny had asked a direct question, he wouldn't be able to get away with a vague answer of nodding or shaking his head. Rather than responding with a shrug or something, Oliver surprised Jennifer by actually speaking. He talked slowly, as if he were trying to articulate his words and make sure they were pronounced correctly.

"The trip was OK. Kind of a long day though."

"I'll bet that you're probably exhausted from everything, aren't you?"

For a moment Oliver didn't respond, and his wheels churned as he tried to process what Granny had just said. "Yeah, I'm pretty tired."

"What is it like in the city where you're from?"

Even though it was an innocent question, it seemed to bother Oliver. Growing slightly pale, he stuffed some pizza in his mouth to avoid having to answer. Granny took the hint and didn't pry any further. There was no need to push that particular subject if he didn't feel comfortable talking about it.

"So, did you find everything in your room and get situated already?"

"Yes, I did," Oliver murmured, finding his voice again. "Thanks."

"That's great. If you need any extra blankets or pillows, just tell us." As Oliver sat there, staring down at his plate, Granny continued to talk. "Oliver, we know this is a hard time for you, but this is your home now, and you can always count on us; we're your family. Jennifer and I are happy you are going to be living with us, and we hope that in time you will grow to love this farm just as much as we do."

Hard time for him? What about me? I'm not "happy" about this new family arrangement either, Jennifer thought, keeping a steady gaze locked onto her cousin.

She doubted that this city kid would ever *love* living on the farm. Most likely, he'd probably stay holed up in his room and would never get within ten feet of the barn, which was fine with her. At least she would have one place to escape to and pretend this whole situation was not happening.

CHAPTER SIX

A new home. A new family. A whole different life.
It was hard for Oliver to digest the things he was being told; none of them were comforting. He didn't want to accept all these changes. All he wanted was to go back in time, to not have to go through all this. Even as the week passed by and settled into the weekend, it was still difficult to come to terms with the fact that he was here. The farm did not feel like home whatsoever. He thought back to the conversation with Granny, having to listen to her say that she was happy that he had moved in with them. How could she possibly be happy about this mess? The word played over and over in his mind, refusing to go away.

How can this be true? Oliver wondered as he stared out his bedroom window. Wishing it could all be a dream, he closed his eyes and shut out the world in a last-ditch effort to escape from reality.

If only it were a dream. If only I could just wake up from this nightmare.

He was almost afraid to open his eyes again, not wanting to accept the truth. But shutting out the world was just as quiet and lonely as being aware. Plus, it was dark, making the distant noise of ringing in his ears even louder. There was no escape. But maybe, just maybe he could open his eyes and everything would be back to normal. Miracles did happen, didn't they? With a deep breath, Oliver opened his eyes and looked around with disappointment.

Still here. Nothing at all had changed whatsoever.

Not willing to dwell on things anymore, he went back to looking out the window again. Unbeknownst to Jennifer, he watched her when she went out every afternoon to ride. Pretty soon it had become a form of entertainment for him. Oliver was intrigued by how well she handled the explosive horse who tended to throw fits every so often. Each ride was different, creating suspense as he wondered how it would turn out. Sometimes Jennifer would have good rides, but on other days, the fractious gray horse would pull every trick in the book to get out of having to listen. When the horse *was* behaving, he and Jennifer were a good pair; they were eye catching as they scaled the hurdles in the jumping arena. It really was something amazing to see.

Today's ride was a bit different; a woman Oliver had not seen before had shown up and was giving Jennifer a lesson. Earlier Jennifer had tried to tell him about her riding instructor, whose name was Annamarie. The woman used to compete in the upper levels in show jumping but had retired from competing and was now teaching. Oliver couldn't remember what rank, or whatever position Jennifer had called it, but from the way she had described things, getting lessons from the woman was a pretty big deal. Apparently Annamarie boarded her old show horse on the farm and gave weekend lessons in return, which was a rare privilege. The only reason the arrangement even occurred was because Annamarie happened to be good friends with Granny. A lot of the stuff that Jennifer talked about didn't make much sense, but hey, it was cool enough just watching from the sidelines. Being entertained by something that could be watched in silence was all that Oliver cared about.

Trying to get a better view, Oliver inched his way to the window and leaned against it, propping himself up on the rough wooden sill. His forehead touched the glass when he craned his neck, completely engrossed by what was going on outside. In the arena, Jennifer had halted her horse and was listening to Annamarie, who was comfortably perched on the fence and talking away, emphasizing with her hands to get her point across.

Being balanced on a tall rail fence like a bird was pretty impressive for a middle-aged woman.

Out of shyness, Oliver had never come out of his room and introduced himself to Annamarie, but from watching he could tell that she was rather gritty yet somehow jubilant as well. She dressed in a funky way. Her collared shirt was blindingly pink, and she strutted around in crisp riding breeches. Although well-worn, her boots were kept clean and spotless. Most noticeably, her black ponytail sprouted through the back of a worn baseball cap, which was black with pink polka dots. It was probably safe to say that Annamarie liked pink.

To Oliver's horror, Jennifer unexpectedly looked up toward the house, and they made eye contact. A sly grin spread across her face as she gazed back at him. Anxious to keep moving, her horse jigged underneath her excitedly. Wondering what the distraction was, Annamarie also tilted her head back to look, seemingly bemused.

Knowing that he had been caught spying, Oliver gasped and ducked out of view. *Jeez, I've been busted!*

What was Jennifer going to think—that he was some sort of creepy stalker? The last thing Oliver wanted right now was to have to explain why he was watching her and Annamarie. He didn't really know why he had been doing it. He just found it kind of interesting to watch Jennifer ride; that was all.

"Who's that?" Annamarie asked. She had not yet met Oliver, nor had she been told much about him.

Jennifer just rolled her eyes and smirked. *What a weirdo.* Her cousin was a terrible spy, thinking that she never saw him up there ogling at them. He acted as if he had no interest in the horses, but she knew better. He was obviously curious about them and peered out the window every afternoon like clockwork. His unexpected curiosity in the horses made Jennifer wonder if there was some hope of them having something in common. Maybe he would be worth getting to know. After all, it couldn't hurt to try; she didn't exactly have a lot of friends who shared her passion for horses. The idea of having a cousin suddenly didn't seem quite so bad now.

Afraid of scaring him off, Jennifer pretended that she didn't see him and kept quiet about it. If there was any way of getting him to break out of his shell, it meant waiting patiently and letting him scrape together enough confidence to come out on his own. Pretty much like gaining the trust of a feral horse that had been through something traumatic. Truthfully, that's what kind of situation this was, come to think of it.

"That's my cousin, Oliver. He had to move in with us."

"Oh, so he's the boy your grandmother was talking about," Annamarie said ruefully with realization. "The car accident, right?" She had found out about that some months ago when it had first happened. But she'd soon forgotten the news as life carried on.

"Yeah." Jennifer sighed and patted Pompeii's neck, and then she ran her fingers through his wiry mane that was peppered with dark gray and white.

"I bet it is a big change for everybody, isn't it?"

You bet? "To be honest, I don't know what to think. Oliver's kind of weird, in my opinion."

This was the most Jennifer had ever talked about her cousin. At first she wasn't sure about telling her riding instructor, but it felt good to share how she felt and to actually have someone listen. Granny never wanted to hear Jennifer say anything negative about the situation, which forced her to box up her emotions and put on a straight face.

Annamarie chuckled. "Really? How so?"

Before Jennifer answered, she glanced up and noticed that Oliver had reappeared at the window. He had that eerie gaze again—his pale eyes were deadlocked onto her like a wolf staring down its prey. Swallowing a lump in her throat, she waved, acknowledging him. He quickly dropped the curtain and vanished again.

OK, have it your way.

"That's what I'm talking about. He never says anything, never comes out of his room, and always *stares*. It really creeps me out!"

Nodding in understanding, Annamarie shifted on the fence to rebalance herself. "He's probably a bit shell shocked. Losing a family at that age is hard, not to mention having to move. Can you imagine having to go through that?"

Hmm, she has a very good point. "You're right. I just wish he would be a little more sociable though."

"Have you tried reaching out to him?"

"Yes, but he ignores me no matter what I do. Did I mention that he's partially deaf now?"

"Deaf?" Annamarie echoed the word with surprise. "Poor kid. You really ought to give him time. He'll come around, I'm sure. But for starters, have you ever figured out if he has any interests, hobbies, or what his old life was like?"

"He clams up whenever I try to ask. I do know that he likes listening to music on full blast twenty-four hours a day, which I find really strange. Only other thing I've noticed is that he likes to watch me ride, so I guess he might be interested in horses, but I'm not sure."

As if struck by some brilliant idea, Annamarie's face lit up. "Then that's what you can use to get through to him."

Confused, Jennifer asked, "What do you mean?"

CHAPTER SEVEN

As simple as it seemed, Annamarie's suggestion was plausible: all Jennifer needed to do was find a way to get Oliver to go with her to the barn so he would be near the horses. If he really was interested, it would be easy to get him hooked. The part of the plan that presented a problem was figuring out *how* to lure the recluse out of the house since he would hardly leave his room. This was going to be challenging.

While busy contemplating and thinking of schemes, including their multiple outcomes, Jennifer studied her cousin, who had come down for lunch. Granny had already left for the day; every summer she did a little volunteer work at the equestrian-therapy camp. During the rest of the year, she helped out with the farm and kept it running whenever Jennifer was away at school. It was just the two of them for lunch, and Oliver was quietly snacking on a sandwich, ignoring Jennifer as she bustled about the kitchen. Every once in a while, he would glance in her direction to see what she was up to. He did appear to be a little curious when she laid out several large bundles of carrots and stripped them of their leaves.

"Hey, *city boy.*" She tried to grab Oliver's attention, but he didn't even flinch. Instead, he sat as if she had not spoken, continuing to eat. Determined to get a reaction out him, Jennifer went over and stood in front of him. His watchful eyes flickered over every step she took. It was the only sign of him noticing her.

This subtle acknowledgment wasn't good enough for Jennifer. Suddenly feeling a bit mischievous, she made a goofy clown face and stuck her tongue out. The bizarre move worked. Taken aback, Oliver tilted his head slightly and arched his eyebrows, as if to say, *What the heck are you doing?*

Jennifer smirked. *Finally, he noticed me!*

⊷ ⊶

I should never have come downstairs.

Oliver felt totally awkward when Jennifer made a face, trying to taunt him, or whatever it was she was trying to do. Wondering what his cousin was truly capable of made him nervous. There was no one to keep her in check today since Granny had gone out to run errands and would not be back anytime soon.

Oliver stared back at Jennifer, ready for any cunning plan she was thinking up in her mind. He knew that if he didn't say anything, she would continue to bother him. If he did relent though, there was a chance she would go away.

"What do you want?" he grumbled as he took another bite of his sandwich. *Can't I eat in peace?*

"I've been thinking…"

Oh no. Don't say that.

"It would be nice if you'd come out to the barn with me. I can show you the horses."

You must be nuts if you think I'm going to agree.

"I think you need to get out of the house. You know, enjoy some fresh air."

No, thanks.

"Besides, I think you'll like meeting the horses," Jennifer added. "I know you've been watching me ride."

Oliver froze at this last comment, unsure of how to react. He'd thought that she had forgotten about the incident, but apparently she hadn't.

Great, now what? "I kind of want to stay inside," he said.

"Why? It's a beautiful day out there."

"Uh, I'm not feeling well right now. I think I'm sick."
OK, that was ridiculously lame.

"You aren't either!" Jennifer saw right through the far-fetched fib.

"All right then, I'll be straight." Oliver sat up in the chair and put on a look of defiance. "I don't want to go outside."

He didn't know if it was an act of desperation or what, but Jennifer reached over and grabbed the back of the chair. Before he realized what was happening, she had managed to drag it away from the table. Oliver accidentlly dropped his half-eaten sandwich as he twisted around to glare at his nutty cousin.

"You *will* go outside."

"Ha, you can't make me."

"Oh, yes, I can!" Jennifer said determinedly. She grabbed Oliver by the arm and tried in vain to pull him out of the chair.

Thinking quickly, Oliver wound his feet around the chair's legs and latched onto the sides with his hands. He'd said he didn't want to go outside, and he'd meant it. He was *not* going. Seeing that tugging wouldn't work, Jennifer tried another tactic. This time, firmly holding the chair, she tilted it backward.

Shocked, Oliver held on even tighter. "Stop it!"

"Will you come outside?"

"No!"

The chair leaned back even more, causing the front two legs to stick up in the air.

"How about now?"

"I'm not going to look at your stupid horses. Forget it!"

Suddenly falling, hands flailing and clawing at anything, Oliver let out an *ooompf* when the chair hit the floor like a brick.

Dang, what just happened?

Jennifer stood over him, smiling slyly. "Sorry, it was too heavy for me to hold much longer, and I got a little distracted when you called my horses stupid."

"Yeah, right." Oliver remained in the chair, refusing to budge. "I'm still not going out."

Not backing down, his cousin grabbed the chair again and flipped it over. By some miracle, Oliver hung on, even though his face was uncomfortably mashed against the floor. Jennifer then began to shake the chair vigorously, so much that he could feel his teeth rattle.

Not—rattle—*letting*—rattle—*go*—rattle.

There was not much he could do though; Jennifer managed to shake him loose and yank the chair away. Without its protection, he started scrabbling away and trying to escape. It was in that moment when Jennifer lost her balance and slipped. She came crashing down on top of Oliver, nearly squishing the life out of him. Luckily, this time the forgotten sandwich that had been dropped on the floor earlier served as a makeshift landing pad.

Oh, the insanity.

Oliver groaned and squirmed out from underneath Jennifer. They both sat up and stared at each other, breathing hard after wrestling. Mayonnaise, bits of bread, and lettuce were smeared into Oliver's hair like paste. A large piece of juicy red tomato was stuck to Jennifer's cheek. *Was it over? Who won?* Oliver waited to see what would happen next. He was bewildered when Jennifer burst out laughing.

"You know, I thought we were nothing alike." She managed to talk between giggles. "We *are* alike. We're equally stubborn, to the point of stupidity. I mean, look at us! We're like two pigs that have just been slopped."

Even though he tried to hold it in, Oliver started to laugh along as he wiped away sandwich remnants. It was a weird feeling: his chest bounced with each chuckle, and the knots in his stomach loosened. He laughed so hard that his cheeks blushed uncontrollably. He'd never realized just how much he missed this. It had been ages since the last time he had loosened up enough to laugh and enjoy a moment of amusement. It really did feel good.

CHAPTER EIGHT

J ennifer led Oliver through the back door of the house toward the barn. They had settled on a compromise. He was free to go back inside and hide in his room, but only after he'd met at least one horse. Fair enough.

The day was sunny and actually kind of cool, despite the fact that it was the beginning of summer. A big oak tree behind the house shaded almost the entire yard. The horse barn was literally standing in the backyard. Now how cool was that?

Just about everyone's dream, to have horses in their backyard, Oliver thought to himself as he stared in awe at the barn. It wasn't a giant barn, more medium size, maybe big enough to hold about six or eight horses.

As they entered the barn, Oliver looked around. The inside of the barn was nice and neat, like the outside. Two horses, realizing that there were visitors, had already stuck their heads over their stall doors and stared at them with anticipation—perhaps hoping to get treats.

Jennifer went over to the first stall on the left, which held a dark-brown horse. She affectionately stroked the horse and fed it one of the carrots she had brought with her.

"This is the oldest horse we have. She's Annamarie's horse—the one I was telling you about. She used to do Grand Prix."

Oliver had no idea what that meant, but it sounded fancy. He reached over and petted the horse's soft, velvety nose and ran his hand over the long whiskers. The mare's face was peppered with gray hairs that blended into the small star between her eyes.

"How old is she?"

Jennifer thought for a moment. "She's about twenty-three."

"Wow, that's kind of old for a horse, isn't it? Pretty amazing. By the way, what is her name?"

"Her name's Valencia," Jennifer replied as she slid the stall's door closed. Seeing that Oliver and Jennifer were no longer going to give her attention, the mare let out a big sigh and went back to dozing in the stall corner.

Jennifer went on to the next stall. A big gray head shot out and snorted loudly. The horse's dark dappled-gray coat glistened in the light that came in through the stall's window as he danced with excitement. Oliver recognized the horse immediately and knew it was the same one he had seen Jennifer riding daily. He was excited to finally get to meet the horse and see it up close.

"That's my horse, Pompeii," Jennifer stated as she calmed the horse by stroking its broad nose.

Oliver eyed the flashy gelding from behind Jennifer. "Pompeii? That's an odd name."

"He is a bit explosive. He's young though. I'm hoping he'll settle down when he matures." Jennifer produced another carrot, broke it in half, and handed a piece to Oliver, instructing him to give it to the horse. "Keep your hand flat, palm up, and fingers straight," she said.

Oliver took the carrot half and did as he was told, placing it in the middle of his hand before offering it to the big horse. Pompeii eagerly snatched it and gulped it down. Oliver was taken aback. "Whoa, he nearly took my fingers off."

Jennifer laughed and continued to pet the horse. "He's kind of feisty, but he's not so bad. When he's behaving, that is." Pompeii nibbled at her hands in search of treats, and she just swatted him away and kept on talking. She was turning out to be quite the chatterbox when it came to horses.

"So, you do show jumping?" Oliver asked when Jennifer stopped talking to catch her breath.

"Yep. I used to compete with another horse, but he has gotten older and is maxed out on his jumping abilities. So he's pretty much retired and just hangs out, getting fat on grain and no work. Granny used to ride him sometimes around the property, but lately she hasn't been doing it as much. He's out in the pasture right now. Anyway, Pompeii is my next step up in the jumping circuit. I'm still trying to work out some kinks, but I think once we start meshing together as a pair, he'll do excellent in the competitions."

"When is the next competition coming up?"

"Well, I'm trying to move up a level, so I won't be competing until I know Pompeii and I are ready. With some luck, we'll be able to enter the Autumn Kellert Show."

"That's pretty cool."

Jennifer continued to drone on about her spectacular horses. She was clearly obsessed with them and really had a strong passion for riding. Oliver didn't mind listening to her talk though. Going to see the horses wasn't as bad as he had expected. In fact, he was glad that he eventually gave in to Jennifer's overbearing request to go to the barn. Getting to look at the horses and pet them had been nice, but Oliver didn't like the idea of actually climbing onto a horse and riding around. That was going a little too far in his opinion. He preferred to keep his feet on solid ground for now. Just the thought of being aboard a moving object that wasn't completely in his control gave him chills. In the past he wouldn't have minded, but things had long since changed.

Thankfully Jennifer didn't ask if he wanted to ride, which Oliver was extremely relieved about. He knew he would not be able to explain his fears if he couldn't even make sense of them himself. No one would ever understand it. Would the crippling paranoia that he faced every day go away over time? He had no idea. He could only hope that it might.

CHAPTER NINE

Triumph. That was the only word that Jennifer could think about while she went about getting breakfast. She had a never-ending sense of accomplishment after successfully dragging her cousin out of the house. As she had suspected, Oliver *did* benefit from the outing, even though he had spent less than an hour in the barn. Now for the first time, he actually stayed downstairs before and after dinner rather than rushing to his room and closing the door as he'd typically done. He also seemed to be a little more relaxed. Even Granny commented on the change that morning before leaving the house, asking Jennifer whether she and Oliver were starting to get along better now.

"Right, make friends with a guy who hardly talks?"

Jennifer rolled her eyes in mock annoyance, trying to hide her satisfied grin. Granny did have a right to be curious, since Jennifer was always concocting some sort of crazy plan. Like the time she jumped out of a tree in order to try to land on a horse parked underneath it like Indiana Jones, which incidentally resulted in a broken arm.

Music suddenly drifted into the kitchen, distracting Jennifer from her thoughts. She turned in surprise and noticed Oliver trundling in, still half-asleep. He had actually gotten up earlier and came down for breakfast on time. It was a miracle! Jennifer wasn't so pleased though when she saw that he was holding his iPod and had headphones sitting crookedly over his head. Even worse, the iPod was playing the same horrid song that she had heard over a thousand times.

Every night since moving in, Oliver would switch on his iPod and let a torrent of music run its course that typically lasted for hours. Or until *morning* if he happened to fall asleep with it playing. She could hear it seep through the thin wall that divided her bedroom from his, and the noise kept her up, making it hard to get a decent night's rest. She didn't know why he listened to so much music. In the past she had thought about asking, but she figured she would not get an answer. Bringing the iPod downstairs was a new one, and

Jennifer was not in the mood to compete with it all day long as well.

"Good morning, sleepyhead," she greeted.

Oliver didn't hear her, of course. By now the chorus of the song was washing away any hope of having a conversation. He drowsily sat down and yawned. When the music finally ended, he turned off the iPod and set it on the tabletop.

"What time is it?" The sentence tumbled out of his mouth like scattered marbles rolling in every direction.

"It's early." Jennifer quickly glanced at the clock that hung on the wall. "Five thirty."

There was long pause as Oliver processed her words, stunned that he had gotten out of bed so early. But he shook it off and asked what was for breakfast. He was always thinking about food, which to him was a priority. *Boys—always hungry.*

"Nothing fancy, I'm afraid. Just plain old cereal."

"What kind?" Oliver mumbled while rubbing sleepy sand out of his eyes.

Ugh, wake up already. Jennifer pointed toward the box of Cheerios that was sitting right in front of her deadhead cousin. He slurred the word *thanks* and fixed himself a bowl of cereal. His table manners had improved a lot lately, since he didn't try to scarf his food down as fast as he could in an effort to escape back upstairs. Now he ate more calmly. He was still a very noisy eater though, unaware that he constantly banged and scraped his silverware against the dishes.

Contemplating different ways to win over her cousin and get to know him better, Jennifer racked her mind for ideas. She'd thought it would be easy, but dealing with this moody creature was much more difficult than handling a horse with a surly attitude. At least horses didn't talk back or glare constantly. Their methods for handling situations were either flight or fight, and they usually chose flight. Oliver tended to rely on silence, refusing to talk or cooperate. This did not faze Jennifer though. Once she set her mind on something, she rarely failed.

One way or another, I'm going to get you on a horse.

Jennifer smirked, relishing her cousin's cluelessness as he looked back at her, perplexed. He had no idea what she was thinking about, and this obviously worried him.

Oliver was finding it difficult to stay awake after having gotten up so early. Jennifer didn't notice it, but he kept nodding off while they ate breakfast. Fearing that he would pass out and end up with his face buried in the bowl, he didn't bother to finish his cereal. Also Jennifer was beginning to make him nervous again, being so unusually quiet and scheming who knew what. Making the decision to split before anything actually *did* happen, Oliver got up from the table and put away his dish. Then he grabbed his iPod and headphones and left the kitchen, all the while avoiding Jennifer's gaze that followed him, studying him and plotting something.

Although he had intended to go straight to his room, Oliver's feet seemed to have a mind of their own. Not sure why, he stepped out the back door and strode toward the barn. It was as if something was pulling him, a yearning inside that reverberated through his senses, robbing him of any control over himself. The barn was a foreign place occupied by large, slightly intimidating horses. Most definitely not a place that he wanted to be hanging out instead of his room.

So what am I doing here? he wondered, strolling down the barn aisle. Maybe it was the longing for peace and quiet somewhere other than his bedroom and away from Jennifer. Being alone was all he really wanted, to escape from the world and drown the ringing in his ears with music. But more than that, he wanted to *forget*—to forget his past, the present circumstances, and maybe even himself.

Deep in thought, Oliver went over to a hay bale that had been left out in the barn aisle. With a sigh, he plopped down on top of it and leaned back against a stall door. The hay was unexpectedly prickly and quite itchy. It definitely wasn't soft and cushy as he had presumed. It didn't bother him much though. He was already beginning to sink down into the hay bale; he switched on the iPod. Once the music started playing, he relaxed and let the lyrics carry his thoughts away. It was his favorite place to be—he was neither here nor there and detached from his surroundings, almost becoming a part of the song and pretending to be in the shoes of the singer. A chance to be someone else with a different lifestyle and no problems to have to deal with. If only that were possible.

As the sky brightened and the sun rose higher in the cobalt sky, the sunlight reached the barn and sneaked through the windows, casting streaks of yellow and orange across floor. They mixed with the shadows and formed scrambled silhouettes. If one had an overly imaginative mind, it would be easy to be fooled into believing that the silhouettes were coming to life as mystical creatures, prowling through the barn in search of a way out before the sunlight obliterated them.

Relaxing in the quiet, yet slightly odorous, horse barn was definitely much more peaceful than being around that lunatic Jennifer. Oliver didn't know that dozing off in the barn would actually be more satisfying than sitting in his bedroom in solitude. Out here, things seemed to be a little more cheerful somehow and less lonely, despite the fact that there was no one around.

Sighing in contentment, Oliver scrolled through different songs on his iPod. He was about to select one when he felt something brush up against his cheek. He jolted in surprise and looked over his shoulder, only to realize that it was just a horse and not some silhouette that had actually come to life. The horse was the color of gold with a white stripe down its nose and stood a little shorter than Jennifer's gelding, Pompeii. It also had a much calmer demeanor as it studied Oliver with dark eyes that reflected the morning light.

"I don't remember seeing you before," Oliver stated out loud.

With a quick glance at the nameplate that hung on the stall, he read the name, *Jasper*. It was fitting, considering the horse's color. Jennifer was obviously pretty good at naming.

When the horse didn't do anything other than stare, Oliver returned to listening to his music. Jasper wasn't interesting enough to keep his attention for long. In a matter of seconds, the curious horse stretched out its head and gently nudged him again. Its warm breath blew across his face, while its long silvery whiskers tickled his cheek. Not that enthralled with horses, Oliver pushed Jasper away. It did little to discourage the horse though. It stretched its head over the stall door and sniffed the back of Oliver's head, sucking his hair up into its large nostrils. It was a creepy, uncomfortable feeling.

"Leave me alone," Oliver muttered while flicking a hand to shoo off the pesky horse. It stopped momentarily but soon tried again, this time pushing its nose against his shoulder. As it explored up and down his arm, it paused and started to investigate his shirt sleeve. Then the horse unexpectedly nipped and pulled at the fabric.

Oliver quickly pulled his shirt loose and swatted at Jasper. "Stop bothering me."

The horse didn't pay any mind to the grumbling and started rubbing its head against Oliver, using him as a scratching post. Sputtering in shock from the weight of the horse's massive head, he shoved it away and stood up. It was clear Jasper was not going to give up trying to get his attention.

"What do you want?" Oliver crossed his arms and glared at the annoying horse. It drew its head back and stared as if it were waiting for something, perhaps a pet or a treat. Starting to get a little curious about the horse, he hesitantly stretched out a hand to see what Jasper would do. He was on guard and ready to yank it away if the horse decided to bite or something. The thought of losing a few fingers was not that appealing.

With its ears pricked forward, the horse eagerly took the invitation and lowered its head, pressing its dark muzzle against the palm of Oliver's hand. The touch was gentle and caring, almost like the good-night kisses his mother used to give him so long ago.

CHAPTER TEN

The splintery wood bit into the skin of Jennifer's arm as she leaned against the barn door for balance. She did not want to risk being seen standing at the entrance and interrupt the private moment that she had stumbled on. She'd never dreamed that she would see something like this. At least, not with her introverted cousin. The horses were due to be fed, but Jennifer was in no rush. There was no sense in spoiling a friendship in bloom, especially when Oliver was showing a different side of himself, opening up for the first time ever. Finally something had managed to penetrate the rock-solid barrier he had built up.

Even though it was slightly dark in the barn, Jennifer could see the emotions Oliver was feeling as he ran his fingers over the horse's face, outlining every visible muscle and vein. Whether he was memorizing all the infinitesimal details or simply enjoying the company, he was completely absorbed in what he was doing.

Being careful not to disturb Oliver and Jasper, Jennifer left her post and went back to the house. It was easy to spy on her cousin since she didn't have to worry about being quiet, as long as she stayed out of sight. She was thrilled to see Oliver reaching out to something other than that annoying iPod of his. After all her planning to lure him to the barn, it turned out the horses had been the magnet that drew him in. The next challenge was to keep everything moving in the right direction. Jennifer began to meticulously construct a plan in her mind to slowly introduce him to riding.

Although older and past his prime, the docile palomino gelding was a perfect match for Oliver. Being Jennifer's first horse, she had learned pretty much everything riding him. Other than competing, he had also served as a companion and friend during her years of growing up, her one constant in life. Maybe now Jasper could become just as valuable to Oliver. That's what he really needed anyway: a friend whom he could rely on without the hardships of communication, a relationship in which words were not needed to be heard or spoken.

There was a sense of nostalgia, an eeriness almost, when Oliver stared back at his own reflection in the bathroom mirror. Leery of what he might see, he had avoided looking at himself over the last few months. It was startling to see how much he had changed since the accident. The person who gazed back at him was unrecognizable, a complete stranger. Although the scars had mostly faded away, there was still a visible mark left behind. It wasn't an old gash or blemish but mostly a mask of sorts, shadowing who he used to be. The healthy color in his face had faded into dull tones, and the vibrant blue in his eyes now appeared gray.

Hoping that his pitiful appearance was just an illusion generated by paranoia and self-consciousness, Oliver glanced down at the two intricate hearing aids soaking up sweat in his hand. There was no denying that he was rather anxious. It wasn't the first time he had dug them out, attempting to convince himself to try them on. Being a stubborn person, he refused to accept his hearing loss and consequently wanted nothing to do with the hearing aids. Furthermore, the issue of having to adjust to them deterred him from making any efforts. He had enough changes to get used to. So the hearing aids usually stayed in the nightstand drawer, unused. However, the daily struggle of not being able to hear was beginning to push his sanity.

Oliver held up the hearing aids and studied them. They were both beige; he had picked out the color in hopes that they would blend in and not be so obvious. Taking a deep breath, he brushed back his hair, which had grown out enough to reach over the tops of his ears. He also touched the hidden welt on the side of his head—the one scar that remained and would probably always be there.

OK, here goes nothing.

The hearing aids felt weird and foreign when he put them on. Most noticeable was the overwhelming noise that flooded in. The disjointed sounds bounced back and forth between his ears. Everything was amplified. Oliver didn't know what to make of it and quickly removed the hearing aids, shuttering the glimpse of an audible life that was literally clutched in his hands. Going from almost-complete silence to hearing again was more challenging than he had expected.

Traveling inside Granny's compact car later that day was like being in a tight prison cell. Actually, it was most comparable to a shark cage, dropped into the water and leaving Oliver at the mercy of the terrors that lived in the ocean's depths. He could feel his profound fear oozing up from the floorboards and lapping over his heavy feet.

Consumed by anxiety, he briefly let go of the door handle and flexed his tingling fingers; then he quickly latched onto the handle again as the car leaned around a sharp turn in the road. Riding in the back of the car was turning out to be overwhelming. The motion of tires rolling over the peppery asphalt and the pull of gravity as the car sped up or slowed down seemed to drag up the dregs of his traumatic past. Too often a memory would be thrust into his consciousness and sting like an unexpected slap across the cheek.

When they began to go straight again, Oliver let out a shaky breath after holding it in—a habit he had when he was preoccupied or nervous about something. It was kind of a stupid thing to do—forgetting to breathe. Feeling lightheaded from lack of air didn't make things any easier. It only made the situation a thousand times worse.

I probably look like a paranoid idiot, he thought. A quick glance at Jennifer, who was sitting in the front with Granny, confirmed it. Her arched eyebrows along with her pursed lips and cocked head begged for an explanation. Oliver could see her curiosity slowly becoming words that tried to inch their way out into the open in the form of a question.

Appearing to swallow whatever she wanted to ask, Jennifer looked the other way. She was overbearing and rather annoying in general, but she had enough consideration not to say anything when Oliver struggled to hold himself together at certain times. Although she had not seen anything yet. *This* was nothing.

Breathe. In and out. In, out, in…

Oliver did his best to steady his emotions, which threatened to spiral into another dimension of lunacy. He could feel himself drowning in his distress, sinking further down with each passing moment. His body became numb under the pressure of the imaginary caved-in car roof. The ringing in his ears got louder, overshadowing the mumbled conversation Jennifer and Granny were having.

Keep breathing, for crying out loud! Why does such a simple task have to be so difficult?

Oliver knew if he kept this up, he would pass out from lack of air. It would be a huge relief though. Maybe it would even make it possible to get out of having to visit his uncle today, whose name Oliver had figured out was Stanley. Granny had gotten a call from him the other day about a shipment that had arrived at his house. It was a box containing some things belonging to Oliver, which they were on their way to pick up. The box was full of stuff that he did not want to see or touch. He didn't even want to know of its existence. He had no clue why his grandmother was insistent on getting the box, but what he did know was that this trip was unnecessary, a complete waste of time, misery included.

CHAPTER ELEVEN

Riding in the car with Oliver was a peculiar experience, and an amusing one too. The way he leaned against the side of the car door as if it were a lifeline while keeping one hand fastened to his seatbelt made Jennifer wonder just what her cousin had gone through. She really did feel sorry for him, but she couldn't help thinking his behavior was kind of funny. Especially when his breaths came out in hyperventilating spurts every few minutes. His face would go from being a normal pink to pale and then blue as he held his breath.

Behold, the chameleon-mutant, Jennifer thought amusedly.

This was way more interesting than the dorky comics she used to read as a little kid. Watching her cousin turn blue like one of those alien creatures from *Avatar* was intriguing. Noticing that her cousin seemed to be on the brink of fainting, Jennifer asked if he was OK. Either not hearing or simply ignoring her, Oliver kept his gaze trained on the floorboards. To get his attention, she reached over the back of her seat and tapped his shoulder. He jumped and let out a whoosh of air like a popped balloon.

Holding back from laughing, Jennifer asked again, "Are you all right?"

Oliver answered with his typical response of nodding, but Jennifer was far from convinced. He wasn't all right at all. Besides, she was no fool. It was clear that he did not want to go on this trip to see their uncle. Even though he did not say anything, the sheer anguish in his eyes spoke volumes. The question was whether he liked Uncle Stanley. Or was it something else?

"Granny, can we make a pit stop?" Jennifer asked when she saw a sign on the side of the road signaling that there was a gas station ahead. She didn't really need to get out of the car herself. It was Oliver who she figured could use a break.

"Sure. There's only about forty minutes to go before we arrive at your uncle's, but we need to refill the tank, so why not?"

"What's going on?" A raspy voice emerged from the back seat when they pulled up to the gas station and parked.

"We're taking a break," Granny replied. "Do you want to get out?"

Do I want to? Heck, yeah! Oliver flung open the car door so fast that it nearly came off the hinges. Caught up in his desperation to escape, he tried to launch out of the seat, but his restrictive seatbelt held him back. Panicking, he wrenched around and broke free of the snare, only to tumble out in a very inelegant fashion. His knees met hard cement as he fell to the ground.

Muttering insolent things under his breath, he scrambled to his feet and hobbled in the direction of the 7-Eleven store that Jennifer had already gone into. The stabbing pain that shot up and down through his right leg did not slow him down. He was already used to his leg hurting every now and then. It was just another reminder of why he had to get away from the car, what had happened to him, and the very reason he did not want to go on this senseless trip.

When Oliver walked through the door, Jennifer bounded over with an armful of candy, crinkling bags of potato chips, and drinks.

"Do you mind taking this stuff to the counter and checking out while I go to the restroom?"

Not waiting for a reply, Jennifer unloaded her treasures into Oliver's arms. Then she took a wadded mess of dollar bills and coins and shoved them into his pocket for him. She showed no regard for personal space. It was country culture to follow the popular motto "What's mine is yours, and what's yours is mine."

Scoffing as Jennifer took off, Oliver juggled the items to keep from dropping anything and carried them over to where the cashier stood. Once the groceries were bagged and paid for, he went back to the car. This time choosing to ride up front, he got inside and hunkered down in relief. He was content to declare that he needed to ride shotgun for a while, not caring about the questioning look he got from Granny or how Jennifer grumbled after finding her seat had been taken when she finally came out of the store. Somehow, being in the front was less upsetting than being in the back, where flashbacks tended to run amok.

Uncle Stanley's house was as bland as Oliver had expected, depicting his unenthusiastic personality. The plain furniture practically dissolved into colorless walls, and the curtains were pulled closed over the windows, destroying any chance of sunlight bringing the dreary living room to life. But it was quirky, too, with a splash of modern art here and there. In the corner was a tall lamp decorated by an extravagant shade made of stained glass, glistening with orange and red swirls.

Another stately piece was a large framed picture displaying a confusing array of splotches that exhibited every color from the rainbow.

Oliver wasn't sure whether the painting was supposed to be some sort of optical illusion or what, but it looked interesting. What really had his attention though was the tortoiseshell cat that sat next to his uncle on the couch. Not caring to make the effort to participate in the conversation between Jennifer, Granny, and Uncle Stanley, he entertained himself by analyzing the cat. It was easy to get lost in those penetrating amber eyes that never blinked. Oliver was reminded of the cat his family used to have, and he wondered what had become of it. Everything had happened so fast after the accident.

Oliver's former home and all his family's possessions had been swept away in a whirlwind of chaos. Uncle Stanley had sold what was valuable and put the earnings in a trust fund, although Oliver did not fully understand all the details. It didn't matter much. Now, he just wanted to get on with the process of picking up the box so he, Jennifer, and Granny could leave. If the others would quit wasting time talking and dithering about, then this would be over with.

When Oliver thought he couldn't take it anymore, Uncle Stanley finally got up and left the room to fetch the container. Soon he returned with a giant-size cardboard box. It took several tries to pack the thing into the dinky trunk of Granny's car, but they finally crammed it in somehow.

About time, Oliver thought when he was able to leave. He was glad to get out of Uncle Stanley's drab house, but it was more discomforting than ever to be in the car, even when he rode up front again. Knowing that the box was resting in the trunk gave him chills. It was an unsettling sensation, as if they were smuggling a dead body or something. Perhaps it felt that way because the items in the box were remnants of his old life—a life that had passed away in a matter of an instant.

CHAPTER TWELVE

There was no way to get around the putrid odor that lingered in the barn. Oliver had a hard time dealing with it, despite hanging around the horses on a regular basis. On the other hand, it had only been a week. Clearly it would take more time to get used to the smell. Today it was more obnoxious than ever, arising from the clumped-up wood shavings strewn with manure. Most of which was stuffed inside a wheelbarrow, precariously balanced on a flimsy tire that wobbled while Oliver rolled it down the aisle. Somehow Jennifer had convinced him to muck out all the stalls, after promising to lend him her computer afterward. It was impossible to pass up on the opportunity to have access to the Internet, a luxury he had been deprived of for too long.

Oliver scrunched his nose in disgust. *Jeez, what do these nags eat?* Although the work had seemed like a really good trade-off, he was beginning to wonder whether shoveling horse poop was worth it.

"Move it along, city boy!" Jennifer said cheerfully. She brushed past in a hurry, dismissing the scowl that answered back. "Annamarie's going to be here any minute, and I want those stalls spotlessly clean before she arrives."

"Bossy..." Oliver grumbled disdainfully when he thought Jennifer was out of earshot.

"What was that?"

"Uh, nothing." *Just saying you're bossy; that's all.*

It was extremely tempting to quit and go back to the house or, better yet, to leave the rest of the dirty stalls for Jennifer to clean. All she did was bark out orders and gripe when the job wasn't being done right. Not only was she overbearing, she was also a perfectionist when it came to horses. An annoying one at that. From Oliver's point of view, good enough was good enough, especially if the job was simply dumping smelly manure into a wheelbarrow and carting it away. Hopefully the privilege of computer access would make up for this torture.

Annamarie arrived just as Oliver was finishing up with the pleasant chores he had been assigned to do. This was his first time actually meeting her in person and watching Jennifer's riding lesson from the arena instead of from the bedroom window.

"So, you must be the new stable hand," Annamarie said after introducing herself.

Unsure whether or not she was joking, Oliver shrugged sheepishly. "I guess so. Jennifer's already taken advantage of the fact that we're cousins and has turned me into her slave."

Annamarie laughed aloud at Oliver's dry attempt at humor. Pristine white teeth showed as she smiled. "Well, that doesn't surprise me. Jennifer tends to be manipulative."

"I'm not either!" Jennifer protested as she walked past with Pompeii. "You're so wrong."

"Ha, I'm most definitely right. You *are* manipulative."

"Whatever." Jennifer waved her hand. "Can you grab my crop for me, Oliver? I forgot it in the tack room." With that, she swaggered off down the barn aisle like the diva she was. Annamarie chuckled and followed her outside.

Doing as he'd been told, Oliver went to go look for the crop. He had no clue where the thing was, thanks to Jennifer's vague instructions. Nevertheless, he still made the effort to try to find it. The tack room was smallish; on one wall was a row of saddles and bridles on racks. An old desk was located on the other side of the room, smothered in clutter that had obviously been left untouched for ages. Next to it was a wooden tack trunk resting on the floor. The lid was caked with enough dust to resemble a minia-ture desert, which deterred Oliver from opening it. There was no chance of the crop being in there. Wondering whether the elusive crop was buried underneath the stuff on the desk, he started shifting stacks of paper, a few moldy carrots, and boxes containing horse supplements—plus some books about riding and other various knickknacks. To his dismay, the crop was not there.

Sighing in disappointment, he gave up looking and put everything back in place. While doing so, something toppled onto the floor by his feet. He stretched down and picked up the object, discovering that it was a small booklet, a journal of sorts. The cover was made out of dark-brown leather, cracked and chafed from age. Oliver opened it and took a peek inside. Interestingly, there was scrawled handwriting on the worn pages, proving that it was a personal journal.

But whose was it? That's what he really wanted to know. Investigating further, he flipped through the pages and read some of the literature, which consisted of information on horses. Whoever owned the journal had spent a lot of time writing down notes. The entries described how each ride had gone, things that had been learned, and tips to remember. Oliver paused at one note and re-read it, enthralled with the small treasure he had found.

March 16
    Today's ride was a new experience, just like every ride is a new journey. With only a few days remaining between now and the next upcoming

competition, the pressure is on. And with my stubborn mule of a horse that somehow decided I needed to fly over a jump on my own today, I've questioned myself whether or not I'm prepared. Truthfully I don't feel prepared at all. The odds are not looking very good so far. Anyhow, this all boils down to this: Is it worth trying anymore? I doubt I'll win anything. After thinking about this, I have come to realize that knowing that I at least gave it a shot will be worth it. Never mind the trophy or the ribbon. If I have a good time and enjoy competing just for the fun of it, then it is definitely good enough for me. Besides, there's always next year. I still haven't quite forgiven Mule Brain for the stunt he pulled though. Still working on that.
—Daniel Murray

When Oliver saw the name permanently printed on the paper, his heart froze. His hands became weak, and he dropped the journal like a hot potato. It landed face-down on the floor, covering up what he had just seen. But it didn't take away the fact that it was there—that name. So terribly missed. Another reminder. It seemed like the memories were everywhere, chasing him relentlessly in a torturous way. Was it too much to ask to forget?

Jennifer didn't know what to think, seeing Oliver tramp out of the barn and head to the house without a word or any other acknowledgment. His faint limp became more pronounced as he took bigger, faster steps. Disappointingly, there was no crop in sight either. So much for that.

"Hey!" Jennifer pulled back on the reins, slowing her horse down to a walk, and called out, "Where are you going?"

Predictably, Oliver ignored her and disappeared into the house. Jennifer knew he heard her because the hobbling rhythm of his stride had faltered for a split second. He even briefly looked back. What on earth was wrong with him? *Weirdo...*

Jennifer rolled her eyes and turned her attention to Annamarie, who raised her eyebrows in puzzlement. "Is he all right?" Annamarie asked.

"Ugh, beats me. He's always doing stuff like that."

"Should you go and check on him?"

There was that familiar question again, those very words suggesting that Jennifer ought to take responsibility and coddle her wacky cousin. It wasn't her problem really. Besides, he had made it clear that he didn't want any consoling. Each time she tried to talk to him, she was answered by a deadpan stare. She had a feeling that he would come around when he was ready, not on someone else's terms, so why force it? Exasperatingly enough, Granny never understood. Jennifer was always left dangling in the middle, being shoved from both sides: Granny would push her to be a friend to Oliver, who always pushed right back. It was a never-ending cycle.

Would Annamarie understand? Jennifer attempted to explain the issue, describing how problematic this *"Check on him. Talk to him,"* drama was turning out to be.

Annamarie didn't get it. Typical adult. "I still think we need to call the lesson quits for today," she said. "Take care of your horse and see what's up with Oliver."

Darn. "Oh, all right," Jennifer resentfully gave in. Thanks to him, the riding lesson was cut short. This had better be worth it.

CHAPTER THIRTEEN

Oliver retreated to his bathroom. Meandering over to the sink, he turned on the faucet and let the water flow at full blast. Droplets splattered against the porcelain, and some sprayed onto the floor. Checking the temperature, Oliver thrust his hand into the stream of water, and to his satisfaction, it was cold. Freezing actually. He splashed some on his face and welcomed the chill. Taking a deep breath and holding it, he then dunked his head underneath the faucet and soaked himself. It was his method of distraction. Anything to get the image of that revolting book out of his mind, even if that meant swimming in frigid water.

To others, everything he did probably seemed like an overreaction. So what? He couldn't help it. Just remembering certain things tended to trap his consciousness and press him into the most daunting corner of his mind. A claustrophobic sensation shackled him, creating an urge to escape. Only there was no getting away from his past. One memory always led to another and another, until he wound up at the worst one—the accident.

In search of her runaway cousin, Jennifer went to the one place she knew he would hide—his bedroom, without a doubt. She pounded on the door vigorously, so loudly that it would be impossible for Oliver to "not hear" her. She wasn't about to let him pull that trick again.

"One moment!" Oliver hollered from inside, clearly flustered.

Not this time, city boy. "I'm coming in," Jennifer replied. Despite the objections that erupted in response, she barged in and then stopped in her tracks and gaped.

Oliver stood in front of her, hair plastered down and dripping water. A million tendrils of soggy strands draped down over his forehead. His shirt was partly drenched too, having gone from medium blue to dark navy. In his hand he was holding another shirt that was dry, which she assumed he was planning to change into.

Looking embarrassed, Oliver walked over to his bed and sat down.

Talk about awkward. Jennifer collected her thoughts, trying to think of what to say. She definitely wasn't going to question why he was soaked or what he had been up to. Acting as if everything were normal, she asked, "So, how are you doing?"

Crossing his arms in defiance, Oliver sniffed. "Everything's fine. You can go on." The sentence almost threatened to end with "and mind your own business."

"But I want to talk things out," Jennifer said, plopping down on the bed next to Oliver. He leaned away slightly and didn't say anything. "You found your dad's journal, didn't you?"

His head snapped in Jennifer's direction, and his mouth fell open in shock. "I thought I put that thing back on the desk."

"Nope, you left it on the floor."

"Oh jeez." Oliver exhaled noisily and stared at the floor. "Now what? Are you going to lecture me about looking through your stuff? I wasn't snooping. The journal was lying out in the open."

"Of course not; why do you think I would mind you seeing it? I actually wanted to say sorry for not showing it to you sooner," Jennifer said.

"What are you doing with it anyway?" Oliver asked.

"I like looking through the journal sometimes to learn how your dad trained horses. This might sound weird, but after reading it all those times, I feel like I kinda knew him."

"Well, at least one of us does! I had no idea he used to ride. My parents never said a word to me about it."

"Seriously? You didn't know about his riding career?"

"Not at all. He must've been good to have written that stuff."

"He really was. I sure hope I can be as good someday."

The conversation dribbled to a close as Oliver sat mulling over what he had learned about his father. Jennifer could tell he wanted to talk but couldn't. His emotions always got the better of him when there was ever any mention of the past. Then Jennifer realized that he did not want to break down in front of anyone. That's why he was so withdrawn. He was afraid.

Seeing that he needed some time alone, Jennifer gave him a pat on the shoulder. "Guess I'll head out. Nice talking to you."

Still caught up in his trance, Oliver remained silent. But just when Jennifer started to get up, he reached out and touched her arm. "Um...wait."

Jennifer turned around. "What?"

With a serious expression, Oliver said, "I want to learn to ride. Can you teach me?"

CHAPTER FOURTEEN

Jasper stood quietly in the crossties while Jennifer helped Oliver to get him ready. While keeping an eye out for any treats that she might offer, the horse's attention was mainly focused on Oliver. It was as if Jasper was sizing him up or something. Being stared at by a horse began to be unnerving after a while.

"I'm not sure this is such a good idea," Oliver murmured.

"Too bad; you're going to ride today. Can't back out now," Jennifer said while she reached for a brush. "Besides, Jasper's a good boy. He'll go easy on you."

What was I thinking yesterday, asking for a riding lesson? Oliver fretted. *And what exactly have I got myself into?*

Jennifer tapped Jasper's rump to move him over. The horse flinched and took a few steps to the side. Without missing a beat, she proceeded to brush him. Not knowing what to do, Oliver just stood there uselessly and watched as Jennifer rhythmically swept the brush over the horse's back. Dust flew up in the air each time she swiped the brush across his coat, eventually forming a cloud.

Suddenly coughing and hacking when he accidentally inhaled some of the dust, Oliver took a couple of steps back. Blowing muck from his nostrils, he glanced at Jennifer, who was brushing down the dirtball. She was still at it, seemingly undeterred by the ominous dust storm.

How can she stand it? Oliver wondered.

Finally, after much effort and time, the dirtball was magically turned into a bright golden-colored palomino. Jennifer stood back and smiled at her masterpiece. Then for a final touch, she grabbed a bottle of spray.

"What is that?" Oliver asked, pointing at it.

"ShowSheen," Jennifer answered.

"What's ShowSheen?"

"It just makes Jasper's coat glossy; that's all."

"Oh, OK. Guess that makes sense." Oliver thought for a moment. Then he asked, "Why do you want to make the horse shiny? I mean, what's the purpose of that?"

Jennifer cast him an irritated look. "Well, duh, I want him to look his best." She squirted the spray onto the horse in short sporadic spurts, leaving large wet splotches on his side.

Holding his hands up in defense, Oliver backed off. "OK, OK, sorry. I was only asking."

"You sure ask goofy questions." Jennifer snickered and headed off to get the tack. A moment later, she came back with a saddle slung against her hip. With her free hand, she handed a bridle to Oliver and instructed him to hold it while she tacked up the horse.

Jennifer quickly settled the saddle on Jasper's back. When she finished tightening up the girth, she said, "I'm going to get a lunge line. I'll be right back."

Compliantly, Oliver stood next to the horse and waited. But then wanting to be of use somehow, he fumbled with the bridle. *Maybe I can help by putting this on.*

By the time Jennifer came back, Oliver had slipped off Jasper's halter and put the bridle on in place of it. He felt immensely pleased with his achievement, especially when he saw Jennifer's surprised look. But it was short lived when she pointed out that the bridle was not on correctly.

"It's on backward. You've got the thing twisted up. How in the world did you manage to do that?"

"Um..." Oliver wasn't sure what to say.

"And I thought I told you to just *hold* it." Jennifer pulled the knotted-up bridle off Jasper, who shook his head with relief.

Jeez, can't I get a bit of credit for trying? Any speck of pride he'd had in his accomplishment was now diminished. Jennifer straightened out the tangled mess that Oliver had created. In a blink of an eye, she had the bridle put back together and on the horse's head, strapped on and ready to go.

Oliver stared in awe. "How did you do that so fast?"

"Oh, it's easy. See, you just have to remember where all the parts go. That piece is called the noseband," she explained as she pointed at the part of the bridle that was strapped around Jasper's nose. "And this is called the cheekpiece; here are the browband and the crown…"

The words floated in the air as Oliver tried to take them all in. It was overwhelming. All these pieces for a bridle? How would he ever begin to remember all this? It must be even harder to remember all the names of a saddle's parts.

CHAPTER FIFTEEN

"This *really* is a bad idea." Oliver managed to spit out the words as he gripped the stiff leather reins in his hands. His fists were clenched around the laced reins so tightly that the laces were leaving imprints in his bare palms. Jennifer had not bothered to give him riding gloves—something that could have been useful at the moment.

Granny had also come out to watch Oliver take his very first riding lesson. As she leaned against the arena fence and sipped away on a tall glass of iced tea, a peculiar smile brought out the dimples in her face, a hint of her expectation that something exciting would happen. Perhaps she was just eager to see whether he'd fall off or not. Not much happened around the old farmhouse, so who could blame her? Oliver had no idea why he had ever volunteered to do this.

Jennifer paid no attention to Oliver's grumbling. Instead she just focused on closing the gate to the arena and securing the latch so it wouldn't open. Then she walked up to Oliver and Jasper. With a smile, she looked up and asked, "How are you doin' up there?"

"Just fine and dandy," Oliver replied sarcastically. "Not like I have any problem whatsoever with being on top of a ten-thousand-pound horse."

Suddenly Jasper thrust his head down and let out a snort. Caught off guard, Oliver jolted and clenched the reins tighter than ever. Rolling her eyes, Jennifer took the black nylon lunge line that she happened to be carrying and attached it to the bridle.

"You know, you are such a stick in the mud. And Jasper actually weighs about one thousand pounds. He's only fifteen hands tall so, he's really not that big."

Oliver glared at her. Why did she always have to be so intellectual with her comebacks? Again, Jennifer ignored him. She took the rolled-up lunge line and started walking backward, stretching it out to its full length. Then she went back over to where the arena gate was and picked up an ominous lunge whip.

"Do we really need that?" Oliver asked as he eyed the whip in Jennifer's hand.

"Sure we do! Jasper's a lazy slowpoke sometimes. So yes, we'll be needing it." Without further mention of the whip, Jennifer picked up the lunge line and clicked her tongue. Jasper sluggishly took a few steps forward and then after a great sigh, slowly set off into the rhythm of a steady walk.

Oliver was pleasantly surprised. *Huh, I guess this isn't so bad after all.*

Getting comfortable, he relaxed and loosened his death grip on the reins. Jasper didn't speed up or slow down as the reins went slack. Instead he eagerly took the opportunity to reach forward with his neck and settled into a nice flowing walk. After about ten minutes of walking in a circle and then another ten minutes of walking in the opposite direction, Jennifer finally decided that it was time to try some trotting.

Of course Oliver hated that idea and protested. "No way. I want to stick to the walk."

"C'mon; it won't be that bad. Just try it once," Jennifer said.

"I said no! And I won't do it. Shouldn't I get another ride or two in before trying something new?"

"Oh, good grief. Let's give it a shot, and if you get scared, I'll get Jasper to slow down to a walk again." Jennifer quickly took up the lunge line and urged the horse forward.

Oliver glowered. "I'm not *scared*; I just don't feel ready. Stop the horse!"

But Jennifer stood her ground and let the horse continue walking. "OK, now get ready to trot," she said. "Sit down on the seat of the saddle and pick up your reins."

Oliver missed most of what Jennifer was saying. All he could catch were the words "get ready."

This is going to be so bad.

Taking on a determined stance, Jennifer raised her whip and flicked it toward the horse. Jasper immediately jumped forward into a brisk trot. Oliver gasped when he was thrown off balance, which was just about as soon as the horse started trotting. In a desperate attempt to stay in the saddle, he dug his fingers into Jasper's short, thin mane. He could barely hang on as he bounced straight up and down as if he were riding a pogo stick, or rather a jackhammer. This was far different from the nice flowing walk. Before he and Jasper could even make full two laps of the circle, Oliver started to lose what little balance he had.

He threw a desperate look at Jennifer and hollered, "Stop the horse! Stop!"

Even though Jennifer started pulling on the lunge line and trying to get the horse to slow down, Jasper kept charging forward. She eventually started to shout something at Oliver. But there was no possible way for him to understand what she was saying while bouncing up and down.

Whatever it was she trying to tell him, it was too late. Oliver lost a stirrup and started falling to the side.

In a panic as he slid sideways, he lurched forward and wrapped his arms around Jasper's slick neck. That seemed to set the horse off. In response, Jasper let out a huge snort and jumped forward into a canter. There was no hanging on. It took exactly three strides before Oliver lost his grip and was deposited onto the sandy ground.

Oliver lay sprawled on his back, gasping for a breath of air as the horse cantered off. A muffled voice called to him a few times, gradually getting louder as Granny made her way into the pen.

"Are you OK?" she asked for the fifth time. She appeared to be concerned, but there was amusement in her eyes when she saw that Oliver was not hurt.

"Ugh," Oliver replied. Somehow despite having had the breath knocked out of him, Oliver immediately picked himself up. There was no way he was going to wallow around in the dirt and let anyone make fun of him for being a sissy. He started to brush himself off in an attempt to regain some of his dignity.

Jennifer came over with Jasper. "Well? Are you OK, or do you need to go to the ER?" she asked impatiently.

"Yeah, I'm fine."

Jennifer smiled. "Good. Let's get you back on Jasper and finish the lesson." She gestured toward the palomino horse that she was holding on to. Oliver could've sworn the devious animal was smiling smugly at him. He was *not* about to ride that cretin again. He felt as if he'd been thrown off a train while it was going a hundred miles an hour. Well, maybe that was an exaggeration, but still.

"No way," Oliver said firmly. "I'm not getting back on."

"Don't be such a coward. Get in the saddle."

"Still not going to."

As Jennifer opened her mouth to say something else, Granny stepped in. "I don't normally interfere when someone else is teaching, but I want to tell you that this is like a life lesson: you can either walk off, or you can face your fears. I recommend you give it another try."

"But—"

"Just one more time. The horse will only walk," Granny said, giving a Jennifer a stern glance.

Oliver finally agreed to get on the horse again, but only on the condition that things would be taken slowly. Under Granny's hard-nosed supervision, Jennifer behaved herself.

Jasper remained calm while Oliver climbed back on. Now that he wasn't being chased with a whip or lugging a clumsy rider around on his neck, he was content to plod around nonchalantly. When Oliver was ready, they did a bit of trotting. It was a much better end to his first ride.

I'm definitely going to ask for another riding lesson, he thought excitedly when the ride ended. He actually wanted to continue, but Jennifer said that it was time for the horse to rest and that he could ride again tomorrow. That seemed like an eternity though. Oliver had had a taste of the horse world, and he wanted more of it.

CHAPTER SIXTEEN

Nighttime came around quicker than Jennifer expected. The horses were already tucked away into their stalls, and the lights were out. Granny had already gone to sleep too. Everybody was tired after such a long and busy day. In the sanctuary of her room, which was jam-packed with horse stuff, Jennifer relaxed under the cozy pink quilt on her bed. A row of stuffed ponies lay by the footboard, their marble eyes observing her. Even though it was kind of late, Jennifer wasn't in a rush to shut things down yet, mostly because she was in the middle of a conversation with her best friend, Lyndsey Evans, on Facebook.

It had been a while since they had talked to each other; her friend was spending the whole summer away on vacation, sunbathing on a Florida beach. Jennifer was a little jealous when she saw the pictures of the crystal-blue water sparkling under the bright sun. The sand was as white as snow. Lyndsey described the texture, saying it felt like sugar.

"That's amazing!" Jennifer wrote on her laptop. "Wish I could be there."

Lyndsey replied, "I wish you could too. They have so many horses here. You'd love it."

Seriously? She had to bring that up? Torture! All horse fanatics knew Florida was a hotspot for equestrians because of the beautiful weather, great land for large riding facilities, and many horses. Swallowing the envy that was rapidly growing, Jennifer decided to talk about something else.

"Yeah, I miss you. When are you coming back home?"

"Hopefully the week before school starts. I can't wait to meet your cousin! What's he like?"

Jennifer paused. She wasn't sure where to start or how to begin to describe Oliver. The last time she had mentioned him to Lyndsey, she'd barely known him.

"Well?" Lyndsey wrote, seeing a delay in Jennifer's response.

"Hmm, he's an oddity."

"Give me more than that! What's his personality? He's a year older than you, isn't he?"

"Yeah, he's sixteen. Very shy and quiet," Jennifer wrote.

"Ha! Of course he is. With your spitfire attitude, you'll turn any guy into a mouse." Lyndsey added jokingly, "I feel sorry for him."

Lyndsey did have a point, Jennifer realized. She was overbearing and wasn't all that sweet toward Oliver when he needed it. He was a city kid, not some rugged farm-boy type, which she typically dealt with around here. Maybe softening her ways would help break him out of his shell. Then Jennifer remembered something. She never did lend her laptop to him like she had promised. Saying good night to Lyndsey, she quickly logged off of Facebook and set out to find her cousin.

Slouched on the couch, Oliver stared listlessly at the television while repetitively flicking through the limited selection of local channels. There was nothing of interest to watch tonight. With everyone asleep, he couldn't turn up the volume enough to hear anything. He did manage to put the captions on, but not without a fight. The ancient television had no ability to function without shorting out or having a spastic fit whenever he touched the remote control. There were a few times he felt tempted to rip those ugly antennas off the squaresville television in protest.

"You're still up? I figured you would be in bed by now."

Oliver looked up to see Jennifer trudging into the living room. "I couldn't sleep," he said with a shrug.

"Is everything OK?"

"Yeah." The automatic answer came out of Oliver's mouth, proclaiming that things were "OK." Truthfully, he was always on the verge of distress. Not that it was anyone's fault. It was simply that he had a hard time accepting his fate and moving on. He couldn't let go of the scenes that played in his mind over and over again, especially in his dreams. He dreaded going to sleep and facing the same replay of events every night.

"Oliver, are you even listening?"

"Huh?"

Jennifer sighed with exasperation, plopped down on the couch, and thrust something into Oliver's lap. "I owe you this."

Taking the laptop, Oliver grinned. "Wow, thanks! I was wondering if I would ever get to use this." For a few moments, he gazed at it, unsure where to start. He had not used a computer in a long time. He had most definitely not been able to get onto the Internet, so it felt weird. What would he check out first? There was a lot to catch up on.

"Well?" Jennifer prodded. "Are you gonna use it or not?"

Jeez, give me a break. Oliver decided to log onto Facebook first. He was dismayed when he couldn't remember his password. *What was it?* he wondered.

After few tries, he got in. He was surprised to find that his Facebook account was flooded with posts, comments, and messages. He scanned his timeline and read some of the things that had been written. They were all saying things like, "Where are you?" or "Where've you been?" or "I heard about accident. Are you OK?"

It was shocking to find that he was actually missed and that people were wondering what had happened to him. Maybe he was wrong in thinking that nobody cared. But was their concern really genuine? Or did they all just post that stuff to look good? None of his so-called friends had ever come to see him in the hospital.

Getting overwhelmed, Oliver scrolled past all the messages and skimmed over some older posts. He paused to look at one of the things that had been posted before the accident: it was a picture of him in his last race. He was passing another runner and about to cross the finish line. His cheeks were embarrassingly crimson red, and his pale eyes were focused as he drove forward as hard as he could.

Oliver almost had a heart attack when Jennifer suddenly pointed at the picture and asked, "Is that you?"

"Of course it is; can't you tell?"

"Sorry, you just look different in that photo."

She's right; I do look a little different, Oliver thought. His hair, bleached from the sun, was a lot shorter then. He had also been muscled and in shape. The racing attire was different too. Jennifer was only used to seeing him in jeans and ordinary T-shirts.

"Why don't you have a computer?" Jennifer asked another question out of the blue. "Didn't you ever have one?"

"Yeah, I have one." Oliver did a mental head slap as soon as he said it. He'd slipped up, releasing a small secret. His laptop, phone, and other belongings were packed away in that box, which he had shoved into the furthest corner of his room.

More questions immediately started to spill. "You have one? Where? Why are you even borrowing mine?"

For crying out loud, please stop prying!

"Did it get lost or something?"

"It's in that stupid box. And no, I don't want to open it right now."

"Oh..." Jennifer quieted. "You really have a grudge against that box, huh?"

"Sorry for snapping. I'm just not ready to deal with it right now. Too many memories."

"Hey, I understand it's hard. I grew up without parents. My father split before I was born, and my mother decided she didn't want me, so I got dumped here. Our grandparents raised me. As you can see, Gramps isn't around anymore."

"That's terrible that your mom left you," Oliver said, a bit shocked that someone could do such a thing.

"Well, my mom didn't technically dump me, but she didn't want to raise me herself. You see, she had me just after she graduated high school, and I wasn't exactly in her plans. Turns out she liked the idea of having a career more than a kid."

"Wow, do you ever see her?"

"My mom used to visit me, but when she finished college, her job took up more of her time till eventually she quit coming to see me at all."

"Where is your mom at now?"

"She's living in England, but I really don't know much about her life. She doesn't stay in touch with me and Granny much."

It had never occurred to Oliver that Jennifer didn't have parents. He had been pitying himself so much lately that he never noticed. They had yet another thing in common as cousins—neither of them could be with their parents. Now he realized there were a lot of things he didn't know about her. He also felt like a bit of a jerk for not bothering to get to know her.

CHAPTER SEVENTEEN

A high-pitched scream sliced through the sound of screeching tires when brake pedals were slammed down. It was quickly drowned out by the crunching noise of metal twisting and gnarling as the vehicles collided, morphing into a mangled heap of scrap iron. The world was then thrown into turmoil, spinning over and over. Shattered glass flung up in the air like glittering confetti. The dark night sky came sporadically in and out of view through the window as the car rolled on the icy road.

Oliver held tight, bracing himself and praying for the roller coaster to end. His seatbelt barely kept him in one spot. The sharp clatter of breaking glass, blaring horns, and metal grinding into the asphalt, along with multiple other disorienting sounds, were cut short when he was suddenly slammed against something hard. Everything blacked out afterward.

There was nothing but darkness. Nothing could be heard. All noise was replaced with a deafening ring, like the feedback of a microphone. The slow realization of being upside down, gravity pulling him toward the car roof, caused Oliver to stir. His movements were hindered, and intense pain ricocheted through one of his legs. Grimacing, he looked up and saw the lower half of his body pinned between his seat and the driver's seat. The caved-in sides of the car obscured everything else in Oliver's line of sight. Hopelessly trapped, he wriggled again in vain.

Unable to hold himself up anymore, he just hung there. Wetness trickled down his cheek and landed on his dangling arm. The dark-red liquid, unmistakably blood, dripped across his shaking fingers. Panicking, he opened his mouth and groaned, but no sound came out. The ringing began to get worse, and dizziness overrode his senses.

Lights—red, white, blue, and yellow—all flashed in rhythm. Orange sparks flew in Oliver's face. Ambulance and police sirens wailed but he couldn't hear anything. There was no sound, just the ringing.

Eventually, the mysterious orange sparks caused the side of the car to split and yawn open. The lights from outside poured in, blinding Oliver. He could feel strong hands grabbing him by the shoulders to support him while his legs were released. Hazy shapes and figures wavered around him as they pulled him out of the wreckage and strapped him onto a gurney. His heart thumped hard, threatening to burst out of his chest, while he struggled to stay awake. He couldn't fight the odd sensation of exhaustion and soon went limp as he fell into unconsciousness, and everything went black once more.

Oliver jolted awake, panting. He was drenched with sweat. What happened? Looking around himself, he discovered that he was in his bedroom. In fact, a small beam of sunlight peeked through the closed curtains. It was nothing more than a horrible nightmare, a past memory of something that had happened ages ago. Breathing heavily, Oliver sat up in the bed and reached for his iPod, which he'd left on the nightstand. It felt cold in his hands. Turning it on, he checked the time. With bleary eyes, he made out the numbers: six fifteen. It was a bit early, sort of. With a grunt, he climbed out of bed. After changing out of his sweat-soaked clothes and getting ready for the day, he made his way down the stairs in hopes that eating breakfast would take his mind off that disturbing dream.

As it turned out, his plan for distraction worked better than he was expecting. Long before Oliver reached the kitchen, he was met by the strong smell of burning food. The odor of charred meat wafted in the air through the house like a deadly poisonous gas. He thought about turning right back around and running for the safety of his room, but curiosity made him proceed, with caution of course.

There in the kitchen was bubbly Jennifer wearing a pink plaid country shirt and threadbare jeans. She was standing at the stove cooking sausage patties—the source of the hideous odor. The sausages weren't the homemade kind; they were the frozen kind that came precooked in a box. This type was meant to be cooked in a microwave, but that didn't stop Jennifer from pretending that she was the greatest chef in the world as she precariously flipped the patties over in the pan. One even flew up in the air and landed with a splat on the kitchen floor, where it bled out a massive amount of grease onto the white tile.

Satisfied that the sausages were cooked—or rather burned into little round black charcoal-like slabs—Jennifer grabbed the frying pan and dumped the sizzling sausages onto a platter, where they lay swimming in a pool of oil. Smiling from ear to ear, Jennifer placed the platter onto the kitchen table. She finally looked up at Oliver.

"Good morning!" she said. "I cooked some breakfast for us. Go ahead and sit down. You don't have to just stand in the doorway."

Oliver hadn't realized he had been hovering there. He had been so caught up watching the horror show in the kitchen that he had forgotten to sit down. "Erm... thanks," he mumbled as he stared at the pile of burned sausages on the kitchen table.

Am I supposed to eat that for breakfast? Bleh...

Not wanting to be rude, he went ahead and sat down at the table. He took a fork and attempted to spear one of the charcoal patties. It took a couple of tries before he was able to pluck the rock-hard sausage off the platter and plonk it onto a plate that Jennifer had already set out for him. By now, Jennifer had gotten her own plate out and was already sawing apart a sausage with a knife.

"So, how'd you sleep last night?" she asked.

"OK, I guess." *Want the real answer? Terrible,* Oliver thought to himself. "How about you?" he asked, in an attempt to keep subjects about him at bay.

"I had a good night's sleep. Can't wait to get my day going. After you eat, why don't you come out with me to the barn, and we can feed the horses?"

"Sure! Want to go out now?" Oliver let out a discreet sigh of relief and got up from the table. He wasn't quite hungry enough to eat those charcoal patties. The girl was a hideous cook. That was the harsh reality of it.

CHAPTER EIGHTEEN

"So, what do I need to do?" Oliver asked when he and Jennifer entered the barn.

"Uh…" What kind of job could she give him? Jennifer hadn't exactly thought everything through when she'd said he could help. She had figured he'd say no.

He must really like the horses. How sweet.

"Why don't you water the horses?" That was a foolproof job. "You can take the buckets from their stalls and refill them. There's a water faucet outside."

Oliver immediately went to work, running back and forth carrying buckets of water while Jennifer managed the food. She was impressed with his efficiency and eagerness to work. Her cousin even hefted a few hay bales that had been dropped off at the barn yesterday up to the loft. Strong muscles in his arms flexed as he effortlessly tackled the chores that Jennifer assigned to him. Oliver was the best stable hand she could've asked for.

Where was he all my life? she wondered. He was a perfect minion. Work around the barn was going to get so much easier as she trained him. Maybe it would be a good idea to suggest to Granny that he needed to start pulling his own weight and help with house chores too. "I think we're done, Oliver. Thanks for your help," Jennifer said.

Not in range to hear her, Oliver leaned over Jasper's stall door, offering a carrot he had snagged from the kitchen before leaving the house. A large golden nose came into contact with his outstretched hand and took the treat. Seconds later, crunching noises indicated the savored consumption of the carrot. Jennifer smiled and turned to go back to the house, leaving Oliver alone with the horse. Inside, Granny was getting ready to leave the house. She looked at Jennifer expectantly as if wanting to tell her something important.

"I've got good news for you."

"Really?"

"A friend just called. They're adopting out some puppies."

"You don't mean…"

"Yes, we're going to go and look at them."

Jennifer almost squealed. She had been wanting a dog for a very long time, constantly begging and doing her best to wear Granny down all year. She was almost ready to give up, but it appeared that all the pleading had paid off. This was it. She was finally getting a puppy!

Oh my God. It's actually happening!

"Thank you so much!" she said, giving Granny a huge hug. She then streaked to the barn to fetch Oliver. Latching onto his hand, she dragged him all the way to the car. There was no time to explain. Her poor cousin was flabbergasted when Jennifer literally shoved him into the back seat.

"What's going on?" Oliver asked as the car rolled out of the driveway.

Jennifer bounced in her seat like a little kid heading to the candy shop. This was too exciting. "I'm getting a puppy!"

⸺⊱⊰⸺

The trip was exhausting. To say the least, Oliver couldn't wait to get back home. Jennifer yakked the whole time. Because he couldn't hear well, her words were a distorted mess, buzzing and vibrating around the tight space in the car. She only stopped talking long enough to coo over the squirming rodent in her lap. A pair of black eyes blinked rapidly, trying to register what kind of netherworld it had fallen into.

"Isn't he cute?" Jennifer wrapped her arms around the puppy and hugged it. Its stubby paws clawed the air.

"Yep," said Oliver. *Keep hugging it. Maybe you'll squish the cuteness out.*

"He's perfect. I've had my heart set on one of these for, like, ages."

"What?"

"An Australian cattle dog," Jennifer explained, misinterpreting Oliver's hint that he had missed what she'd said a minute before. "They're a hardy breed, good for herding."

"Oh."

"We need a name for him."

"How about Red?" Oliver suggested. The puppy was the same color as Jennifer's hair, unsurprisingly.

"Too boring."

Granny threw in a name idea. "Rascal?"

"Maybe. Kind of common though."

"Creature?" *He looks like a little gremlin with those big ears of his.*

"Oh, I like that one!" Jennifer threw an appreciative glance in Oliver's direction. "It fits him."

Oliver smiled back, pleased that she liked the name. Every day they seemed to be more agreeable with each other and, dare he think it, closer as a family.

CHAPTER NINETEEN

The house was quiet during Saturday. Jennifer played with her new puppy outside, and Granny sat in the living room, reading her favorite bird-watching magazines. She had a stack of them on the coffee table that she had not yet had the chance to look at. With the summer coming to an end, she was finally able to be home again during the weekends.

This gave Oliver the opportunity to try something while nobody was watching. Slipping his hearing aids on, he inconspicuously wore them around the house and tried to get accustomed to how they worked. It was nothing like what he was used to. Everything sounded electronic and a little too noisy. Nevertheless, it was a blessing to hear so much at once. For the rest of the day, he rediscovered various sounds that he had not heard in a long time: the repetitive squeak of the living room's swirling ceiling fan, the drone of the refrigerator in the kitchen, birds chirping outside, Jennifer laughing as her puppy barked playfully, and so much more.

These hearing aids really do work, Oliver noticed. *Why didn't I start using them sooner?*

Suddenly the back door flung open, screaming in agony as it smacked against the wall. Jennifer barreled into the house with Creature on her heels, her wild Medusa-like hair going in every direction. Both Granny and Oliver were startled by the abrupt chaos coming from the kitchen. Creature ran through the hallway, skidded around the corner, and dived toward Granny's feet. She let out a yelp as he squirmed and wriggled his way between them until he disappeared under the chair.

Targeting Oliver, Jennifer bounded over. "It's getting extremely windy outside!" she hollered at the top of her voice, not knowing he had hearing aids on. "I think there's a storm coming."

Oliver flinched and took a step back. Jennifer had been practically yelling at him all this time, and he hadn't even known it.

"Can you help me get the horses into the barn?"

"Yeah…"

"Hurry up! I don't want to get caught in the rain!"

"Be careful out there!" Granny called after them, also raising her voice. "I'll come help once I get the laundry off the clothesline and the windows closed in the house."

Wow, she's been speaking loud too. Oliver was shocked. They had both been making an effort to help him hear them.

The horses were in a frenzy, scattering across the pasture. Their manes and tails whipped around in the wind. Frantic neighs rang out as they paced the fence line. Raindrops were already starting to descend from the gray sky. Within minutes, the storm had worsened. Gathering up some halters, Jennifer chucked a couple of them at Oliver. She pointed to one of the horses, Annamarie's mare, and said something.

"What?" Oliver was deaf once again. His hearing aids were rendered useless outside; the wind sounded like a whirring blender.

"Get Valencia and Jasper!" Jennifer yelled over the wind. "I'll grab Pompeii. He's harder to catch."

Nodding in understanding, Oliver took the halters and went for Valencia first, who was easy to get a hold of. Eager to reach the barn, she practically led the way. As soon as the old mare settled into her stall, she dropped and began to roll in the dry bedding. Jennifer was still chasing after Pompeii when Oliver headed back outside. Refusing to be caught, the rebellious horse galloped back and forth in the pasture, and Jasper kept having to skitter out of the way to avoid getting run over.

Oliver decided to try to fetch the disoriented palomino, presuming that if he removed the horse from the pasture, it would give Jennifer more room to catch Pompeii. He dashed across the pasture with a halter in hand. After dodging Pompeii multiple times, Oliver quickly haltered Jasper, and then, bracing against the howling wind, he trekked toward the pasture gate with the horse following behind him. Rain spattered on the writhing grass. Trees leaned and groaned. In the distance, he could see the lit-up barn glowing with the essence of a lighthouse.

Like a storm cloud, Pompeii stampeded past and then skidded to a halt. His eyes rolled hysterically as he reared up, towering over Jennifer, who was in his path. She remained steadfast, unfazed by the flailing hooves. Out of nowhere, a loud crack of thunder shook the world. Alarmed, Pompeii immediately returned to earth and spun away, leaving deep grooves in the soggy ground.

"Look out!" Jennifer cried in horror when the horse bolted toward Oliver and Jasper. It was too late to move though.

The violent impact of Pompeii's broad chest, packed with unrestrained strength, knocked Oliver facedown into the mud. A hoof slammed down onto his shoulder, just inches away from his head. He was too shocked to feel it. Angry squeals erupted when Jasper kicked at Pompeii, fed up with his antics, and pretty soon they were lunging at each other with bared teeth. Struggling to get out from underneath the two quarreling horses, Oliver scrambled around their stomping hooves. But before he could get up, he was stepped on again, this time getting caught in the ribs.

Crud!

Seeing stars, Oliver clambered to his feet and escaped. The adrenaline that surged through his body did little to mask the pain. Jarred from the ruckus, his bad leg throbbed with a vengeance.

That's it, I've had it with those dang horses! I'm done!

Jennifer lunged into the fray and grabbed the lead rope attached to Jasper's halter. Trembling from the frightening close call, she glared after Pompeii as he ran off again. The stupid horse could've killed Oliver. No more pasture time for that beast. Her attention then went to her cousin, who was stumbling around in a drunken way. Squinting to see through the drizzling rain, Jennifer asked if he was all right. Everything had happened so fast that she wasn't sure whether he was hurt or not.

Oliver stopped and glowered. That was when Jennifer got a glimpse of his face, caked with chocolate-colored mud. The only thing visible were his saucer-shaped eyes, bugged out and furious.

"Am I all right? Heck no!" He keeled over and spat out a gob of mud he had swallowed.

"How badly are you hurt?"

Rather than answering, Oliver surprised Jennifer by swearing a couple of times and staggering out of the pasture, muttering that he was never going to help with the horses again.

So much for my personal stable hand, Jennifer thought. *Can't exactly blame him after that ordeal though.*

Tired of trying to chase down Pompeii, Jennifer gave up and left him in the pasture. She figured that if he was so dead set on staying out in the rain, then so be it. Also the storm was starting to die down, so it didn't really matter so much now to bring him in. He'd be a mucky mess later, but she didn't care anymore.

After putting Jasper away in his stall, Jennifer hurried to the house to see if her cousin was still alive. When she came in, her worries eased a little once she saw Oliver in the living room. He was seated on the coffee table with his arms crossed and showing his resentment with an indignant scowl while Granny checked him over meticulously.

"Hey." Jennifer approached cautiously, unsure whether or not he was still upset. "I took care of Jasper."

Oliver grunted, testifying that he couldn't care less.

Yep, he's definitely mad.

Granny shot a fleeting glance at Jennifer—a subliminal message that an explanation was owed. "I don't know what you two were up to, but y'all certainly didn't listen to my warning, I can tell that much."

"It was Pompeii's fault." Jennifer jumped to defend herself. "He spooked."

"He didn't spook; he tried to kill me! I might've died," Oliver protested.

"Come on; it wasn't that bad."

"Oh yeah? Why don't you just go out and let that thing stomp all over you? See if it isn't that bad."

"He's not a *thing*. His name's Pompeii!"

Waving her hands, Granny interrupted them. "That's enough. I don't want to listen your squabbling."

"He started it!"

"I said that's enough!" Granny put her foot down and continued to assess Oliver. She lifted the back of his shirt, revealing a perfect horseshoe print on his shoulder. It was large, most likely left from one of Pompeii's big hooves.

"Does that hurt?" A devious streak overpowered Jennifer's last remaining bit of sympathy. She reached over and poked the bruise with her finger.

"Ow!" Oliver pulled away. A murderous glint in his eye warned her not to do it again.

Trying her best to ignore the nonsense, Granny sighed. "I don't think anything's broken. You're lucky, Oliver. Sinking into that mud probably saved you from getting crushed."

Jennifer shuddered at the thought of her cousin being turned into a pancake. That would've been pretty bad.

"Anyhow, I'm going to go and find some painkillers for you. Hopefully it will take the edge off." With that said, Granny left the living room.

Now alone with Oliver, Jennifer looked at him, wondering if he would start griping about the horses or, worse, blame her for everything that had happened. But he didn't. Instead he just kept his thoughts concealed and wiped at his face, pessimistically streaking the mud across his cheeks. He was in a pretty pitiful state, battered and bruised like a rag doll that had been smeared into the dirt by a steamroller. No doubt he probably felt that way.

Feeling bad for him, Jennifer apologized. "Sorry you got hurt. I wish I could've prevented all this."

For a few lingering seconds, Oliver didn't utter a word. Finally, he simply smirked at her.

"What?"

"It's nobody's fault. It was an accident." Oliver started to chuckle at the absurdity of everything. "Besides, I've won the jackpot of pain. Not many people can outright say that."

Jennifer began to snicker as well, although she had a nagging feeling that his statement had a deeper meaning somehow. What exactly was he trying to point out?

CHAPTER TWENTY

The days went by slowly and rapidly at the same time, if that was even possible. Summer was drawing closer to an end, which meant Jennifer would be going back to school soon. Granny had decided to let Oliver homeschool for now, saying she felt that he needed just a little more time to settle in. Oliver didn't know how to feel about any of it. He just wanted life to get back to normal, or rather as close to normal as things could get under the circumstances. At the same time, he felt anxious about the idea of attending public school. How would people react to him? How would they treat him? Would they think he was weird and make fun of him? What would they say? There were so many questions.

The worst fear Oliver had about going to school was the fact he wouldn't be able to run on the track team, which was one of the only things he was actually good at. His hearing wasn't the only thing that had been damaged in the accident. It also left him with a shattered leg that had never fully healed, even after having surgery to repair it. Technically he could still run, but he wasn't anywhere close to being fast enough to win races. The glory days were over for him. Running competitively was no longer an option. It was a pretty depressing situation, having that particular dream smashed.

After mulling over all that he had lost, Oliver began come to terms with the issue that he needed a new hobby, anything to keep himself busy. So he supposed, why not horses? They could be his next full-time occupation to fill in the hole where his passion for running had once been. He was about to go berserk in this boring farmhouse anyway. It would only get worse when Jennifer went off to school. He entertained the idea of asking Granny to help teach him to ride. Now that she wasn't busy with volunteer work, she had free time on her hands. But he still preferred Jennifer much more when it came to learning about horses. Either way, he had to decide sooner or later before he died from boredom. Desperately needing a change in routine, Oliver dawdled in the barn despite asserting that he absolutely hated horses now. But he was slowly beginning to forgive them after taking a few days' break from riding.

Pompeii was still blacklisted though. That horse was an imbecile. A rock would've been more intelligent.

Oliver meandered up to the stall of the horse he did sort of like. Leaning over the wooden door, he gazed thoughtfully at Jasper, who was busy munching away on some hay. Every once in a while, the palomino gelding would swish his cream-colored tail in an effort to deter the flies that hovered in the air. He never bothered to notice the person observing him, even when his name was called.

Using his fingers, Oliver drummed the top of the stall door to catch the horse's attention. Curious about the new sound, Jasper lifted his head and blinked but still didn't come over.

OK then, ignore me.

Out of the blue, a voice interrupted the calm tranquility, and with a touch of amusement, it said, "I wasn't expecting to find you out here in the barn." Whipping around in shock, Oliver nearly collided with Jennifer. She had been standing right behind him without him knowing it. Stepping back, she apologized. "Sorry, I didn't mean to scare you."

"Well, you kind of did," Oliver said. He scratched the back of his head, still trying to figure out how she had managed to sneak up on him so easily. He was used to wearing his hearing aids now and was surprised he had not heard her approach. Unfortunately, they weren't quite infallible. Although the loudness he had experienced in the beginning was just an illusion, after everything having been so quiet, his hearing loss wasn't cured. However, the hearing aids certainly still helped in many ways.

"So what are you doing in the barn? I thought you didn't want anything to do with horses."

Shrugging indifferently, Oliver leaned over the stall door again. "Just bored out of my mind. I needed something to do."

"Oh…" Jennifer cocked her head and thought for a moment. "Would you like to give Jasper another try?"

"I don't feel like riding."

"Oh, no riding. We could try somethin' different this time."

"Like what?"

The new idea that Jennifer had was quite interesting, and it was a very different approach than what Oliver had expected. Instead of tacking up the horse, Jennifer simply haltered Jasper and led him out to a small round pen that was hidden on the back side of the barn. The only equipment she brought along was the same lunge line that she'd used in the first riding lesson.

"What are we going to do?" Oliver questioned, keeping a wary eye on Jennifer, who flashed her signature smile at him, the one that meant she was up to something.

"We are going to lunge."

"Lunge? What is that supposed to mean?"

"It's an exercise that's commonly used with horses," Jennifer explained while she slowed to a stop. Still holding onto Jasper by the lunge line, she reached across with her free hand and pushed the gate closed. "Basically you run the horse in a circle around you, if that makes sense."

"Actually, it doesn't."

With a chuckle, Jennifer unclipped the lunge line from Jasper's halter and allowed him to roam free in the round pen. "You'll have to see it to understand."

What if I don't want to see it? Oliver thought anxiously. Being around Jennifer was like playing with matches. If he wasn't careful, he'd end up in some crazy mess. But curiosity got the better of him, so he went with the flow and let Jennifer show him her great idea.

Still keeping a close watch on Jennifer, who was coiling up the lunge line, Oliver turned and climbed on top of the fence rail so he could sit down and watch. Slightly bored, he began to bounce his legs like a toddler would as they dangled over the side. Tilting his head forward, he noticed that the hems of his jeans were stained with dirt. So were his black tennis shoes, which were colored in various tones of gray and brown from walking around outside near the horses. It was still an unfamiliar sight, seeing his shoes all dirty. In the city where he came from, they had never seemed to get quite so dirty.

Realizing he was busy looking at his shoes and not paying attention to what Jennifer was doing, Oliver quickly looked up in time to see a blur of gold rushing past. Bits of sand and dirt flew up and pelted him in the face when the horse threw in a lively buck as it galloped by. Wiping the grit off his cheeks, Oliver squinted his eyes and watched the demonstration.

Jennifer was in the center of the round pen with the lunge line still in her hands. Every once in a while, she would flick the end of it at Jasper to keep him going. A few minutes went by, and Jennifer finally let him slow down to a walk. The horse lowered his nose to the ground, snuffling the sand in search of grass, and nibbled on an isolated weed that had sprouted under one of the fence boards. He always seemed to be hungry.

"Do you wanna give it a try?"

Oliver froze, unsure of what to do or say. "Um…" *Don't do it. Danger alert!* his senses screamed.

"Come here," Jennifer coaxed, motioning him to leave his perch on the fence. Hesitatingly, Oliver climbed down. He trundled over and took the lunge line she was holding out for him.

What are you doing? This is a bad idea. Run away!

"What we're about to do is something called a join up."

"What's a join up?" *Make a break for it while you still can.*

Suddenly sounding knowledgeable and sophisticated, Jennifer replied, "It's a technique that is used to help bond with your horse. A well-known trainer named Monty Roberts does it a lot with different horses when dealing with trust issues. I'll coach you through it. I think this is what you guys need to get along. Jasper needs your trust, and you need his respect."

"Sounds complicated," Oliver said.

"It's not. Just give it a try and see what you think of it."

Even though Oliver was not totally sold on Jennifer's plan, he went ahead and obliged, doing what she said. Surprisingly it wasn't that hard after all. In fact, it was rather fun and entertaining; before long he had Jasper cantering in a circle around himself. It only took a flick of the end of the lunge line and some encouragement with his voice to get the horse going.

Sometimes Jasper would throw in a couple of hops and toss his head, just to show he wasn't quite ready to pay attention to Oliver. Suddenly his tail stuck up in the air and he bolted forward, churning up sand with his pounding legs. All the while, he turned his head slightly to the side, keeping a gaze of defiance trained on Oliver.

Hmmpf, I can play that game too, Oliver thought cheekily as he flicked the end of the lunge line again, almost touching the horse's rump. Jasper hastily responded by kicking out. *Really?*

"Hey, you need to drive him forward, not torment him! This isn't a standoff," Jennifer lectured from the sideline. "See if you can get him to go the other way again."

Rolling his eyes at Jennifer's nitpickiness, Oliver stepped forward as he had been taught to do, moving toward the front of the oncoming horse. For a second he held his breath when he noticed Jasper wasn't slowing down. In the last second though, Jasper finally registered Oliver's presence and balked. His muscles bunched and rippled as he skidded to a partial halt and spun around so he could go the opposite direction. Breathing a sigh of relief, Oliver returned to the center again. His heart thudded in his chest from the rush of adrenaline. He barely heard Jennifer's muffled voice calling out to him.

"Do you see his mouth, how he looks like he's chewing?"

Looking closely, Oliver saw what Jennifer was talking about; Jasper was opening and closing his mouth in a chewing motion, as if he were munching on grass or something. What did it mean? Was he hungry again?

Finding it difficult to talk and concentrate at the same time, Oliver answered with a nod. It was hard enough twirling round and round in a circle and trying not to get dizzy while lunging the horse. He was beyond glad when Jennifer told him to stop and stand still. No more mindless spinning in circles. Now that he was no longer being driven forward, Jasper transitioned to a walk. His sides puffed in and out from all the running.

"Now turn away and pretend he's not there," Jennifer instructed.

"Why?" Oliver questioned. He didn't feel good about turning his back on the horse, nor did he trust Jennifer. She had already got him into trouble more than once.

"Just do it!"

"OK, OK." Taking another deep breath to control the rush of nerves that surged through him, Oliver did as he was told and moved so he was facing away from the horse. He kept his eyes focused on the ground, studying the hundreds of footprints that he had left in the sand after twirling in a circle for the past hour. Most of them overlapped one another. Some meandered outside of the hodgepodge of footprints, showing where he had occasionally stepped toward Jasper to get him to change directions.

Before long, Oliver felt small vibrations under his feet as Jasper's hooves treaded behind him. Then he felt a soft, sultry breath blow onto the back of his neck. The breeze ruffled his shaggy hair.

What should I do? he wondered as he fought the urge to look over his shoulder.

Breaking the silence, Jennifer finally said, "You can give him a pet now."

Turning slowly, Oliver came face to face with Jasper, who calmly gazed back with large dark eyes, his ears swiveling back and forth like antennas.

Oliver quietly stroked the horse's nose and idly ran his fingers along the side of the white stripe that streaked down the middle of it. There was a certain sense of serenity, a sort of peace hanging in the air between them; here Jasper was, actually coming to Oliver for once. It was almost like the horse was ready to listen, to be his friend and companion, and was willing to be there for him, not just for treats but because he wanted to.

CHAPTER TWENTY-ONE

"I've got someone for you to meet," Jennifer said the next morning, going on to explain that she had a friend who had just come back from vacation and was coming to visit. Oliver presumed he would simply meet the friend and then go on about his day. But boy was that an underestimation. The girl was a chattering loon when she arrived at their house. She was full of excitement and her eyes were enlarged behind red-rimmed glasses.

"Hi! I'm Lyndsey!" she screeched with exaggerated enunciation, thinking it would help Oliver understand her. "Jennifer's told me all about you."

Maybe a little too much about me, Oliver thought as he winced at Lyndsey's encroachment into his personal space.

"I've been dying to meet you. Wow, you really have the palest eyes, don't you? They're like crystals."

"Oh."

"I also heard you're hard of hearing. Were you born that way?"

"Just partially, and no." At least Jennifer had been considerate enough not to mention every single detail.

"So what do you think of living out in the country? Pretty cool, huh?"

"I guess."

"How long will you be staying?"

"For a while, since I live here now."

"Are you going to be attending school next week?" Lyndsey spewed, opening and closing her mouth in an unnatural way, as if she were trying to vomit the words onto Oliver's face. Somehow she assumed that it would help him understand her. "If you are, I hope you're in my class."

Jeez, I certainly hope not.

"What kind of things do you excel at—sports? You look athletic."

Struggling to keep up, Oliver failed to answer the questions. "I uh, yeah." *Please slow down!*

"Are you going to enroll in school? Awesome, I can't wait to see you there!"

"No, I meant—"

"I remember Jennifer telling me that you ran track. The team could really use a good runner. The guys at school are hopeless slugs."

"I can't run anymore," Oliver blatantly stated. Jennifer, who was standing nearby, raised her eyebrows in surprise. He hadn't bothered to mention it to her before, since she never asked. Plus, it didn't seem necessary to rehash that gloom. Lyndsey was also slightly taken aback, seemingly embarrassed as she resisted asking why. Brushing her dark frizzy hair back, she initiated another topic.

"Oh, that's too bad. Do you ride? I bet Jennifer's had you on a horse by now."

"She has—"

"I knew it!" Lyndsey interrupted again. "Keep riding, bud. I bet you'll be good at it, like your dad was."

"Um—"

"Have you ever seen pictures or videos of him riding? They're all over the Internet."

Oliver began to get increasingly uncomfortable as the gap between him and Lyndsey narrowed. Her obnoxious voice rattled his eardrums, deafening him even more. He could manage to handle that part somewhat, and even the onslaught of questions. But talking about his father reached past the limit.

⊷ ⊶

Seeing the tension rising in her cousin, Jennifer tried to intervene. "He hasn't seen them yet. Maybe sometime I'll show him."

"How about now?"

Jennifer flinched, wishing her friend would let it go. Lyndsey was so clueless when it came to sensitive topics.

"No, later." Oliver's lower lip was turning blue as he bit it in an attempt to hold himself together. His weight shifted from foot to foot constantly. All these signs were like huge red flags being waved frantically.

"Aw, OK." Lyndsey sighed. "It's too bad Daniel passed."

Oh no. Jennifer knew where this was going.

"It was such an unfortunate thing that happened to your family. I've heard they were—"

"Stop!" Oliver suddenly blurted, his face turning beet red. Veins pulsed in his neck. "Just stop! I don't care about what you heard." Not waiting around, he turned and stormed off.

Well, Jennifer didn't exactly see *that* coming.

CHAPTER TWENTY-TWO

Jennifer's profuse apologies seemed to ease Lyndsey's bewilderment. Luckily, she never held grudges and forgot about the incident in less than ten minutes. Thank goodness. The girls spent the rest of the visit chatting about the Florida vacation and plans for school stuff. They also fawned over Creature for a good long time. Nothing could out-cute that puppy. But even his cuddles and playfulness didn't brighten Jennifer's mood much. As soon as Lyndsey finally left to go home, Jennifer hunted for Oliver, ready to chew him out for his cantankerous behavior. She was tired of the nonsense. Sure, life hadn't been easy for him lately, but it was time he got over it. There was no need for him to take his frustrations out on others.

"Oliver!" Jennifer hollered when she found him. She had searched the whole house and barn. Of all places, he was in the tack room, sitting on the floor with his headphones on and music blaring. Comfortably hunkered down in the far corner of the back wall, he had been out of sight when Jennifer had opened the door once before and peeked into the tack room, but she'd finally spotted him after checking a second time.

"I don't know what came over me," he said apologetically as he quickly removed his headphones and turned off the iPod. He looked up at her with wide eyes when she stomped over and glowered down at him.

"Stupidity, that's what came over you! Why'd you snap at Lyndsey?"

"I'm really sorry."

"Do you know how embarrassing it was?"

"I'm sorry," Oliver repeated again.

"Seriously, that's all you can come up with? Ugh!"

This time Oliver kept his mouth clamped shut and stared back expressionlessly. As usual, he was withdrawing into himself, a last-ditch effort to get out of a sticky situation. Basically shutting down so the conversation couldn't proceed.

Irritated, Jennifer jabbed him hard in the chest with her finger to rouse him. "Come on, talk!"

Oliver pushed her hand away and didn't yield to her request, so Jennifer poked again, even harder. Good grief, he was stubborn. Why did they have to be so alike in that way?

Scowling, Oliver snapped, "What do you want me to say?"

"Anything! You always refuse to share what's on your mind. How can I tell what's going on if you don't let me in every once in a while?"

"There's nothing I want to talk about."

"Exactly. You're being difficult. If you'd just speak up, maybe I could help to prevent situations like the one with Lyndsey. Then you wouldn't have to go around having these dumb outbursts. They're getting old."

"Look, I can't be helped. Do you really want to know about my problems? OK then…" Oliver bent over and pulled up his right pant leg, peeling it back over his knee. A wicked set of scars branched around his shin and across his calf. Some were caused by injury, and others were surgical.

"Is that why you can't run?" Jennifer cringed as she wondered how it must've felt.

"I almost lost my leg when it was crushed in the accident. It's held together with pins now. I can't race anymore. Happy now?"

"I had no idea." No wonder he'd started getting upset when Lyndsey talked about the track team. To not be able to do what he loved had to be torture.

"Want to know more?"

"No, it's OK. You really don't have to."

Ignoring Jennifer, Oliver pulled something out of both his ears and showed her a pair of hearing aids. "I just recently started wearing them. I didn't say anything, because I was worried that you and Gran would stop speaking loudly."

"Whoa, how many secrets do you have?"

"I have lots of secrets. Ha, you hardly know me!"

"Like what?"

"Well, did you know I had a sister? Her name was Emma, and she was just ten years old."

Oh God, I've just opened Pandora's box. What have I done?

"Flashbacks seem to be a daily part of life now. I can't remember the week before the accident, but lucky me, I can remember every single detail of the wreck, getting to relive it again and again every night when I go to sleep. It's not only dreams but also memories of what happened after that, like sitting at the funeral and having to see my whole family buried all in the same day."

"I'm sorry." It was Jennifer's turn to apologize. What else could she say? Suddenly she was in way over her head and had no idea what she should do.

"And why am I so quiet? Have you ever considered that I have a hard time following conversations? I literally have to repeat each sentence in my head and make sure I heard it right. It's like piecing together a puzzle, guessing the missing words. When I'm focusing that hard, I don't have time to think of how to answer."

"Earlier you were just trying to ignore me. Don't deny it."

"Yeah, I was, but I mean in general. I've never complained, but I always feel left out and excluded. For example, at dinner when you and Gran are talking, it's exhausting just trying to keep up with your conversations, not to mention trying to participate."

Holding her hands up in defeat, Jennifer said, "I get it; it's not easy, and it stinks. I understand completely."

"No, you don't." Oliver gathered his things and got up off the floor. "You'll never understand my problems. You'd have to experience them yourself to get an inkling of what it's like, to know personally, and deal with it each day from sunup to sundown. No matter what I say to you, nothing's going to change. It won't make a difference for me."

"Surely talking things out would help somehow. I'm always ready to listen. See? I'm paying attention right now."

"Do you really want to help? Start by allowing me to keep things to myself. Quit asking if I'm OK, what's wrong with me, and why I spaz out sometimes. You can't rehabilitate me like some animal you rescued from neglect; only time will."

Jennifer was at a loss for words. The dam had unexpectedly broken, and her cousin was spilling his thoughts, but she wasn't prepared for it. All her previous attempts to crack him open had been rejected. Part of her wanted to believe everything he said, but doing nothing sounded unreasonable.

"Remember that lunge lesson about trusting the horse?" Seeing Jennifer's doubtfulness, Oliver stared deep into her eyes, searching for a way to drive his point home. "Please trust me on this. I need to get through my problems on my own."

CHAPTER TWENTY-THREE

"Oh, Granny, I don't know what to do anymore!" Jennifer moaned after having confided in her grandmother, relaying the whole tense conversation she'd had with Oliver. She had to do something; things were very awkward between them lately, and living in the same house didn't help. This morning Jennifer was about to leave for the first day of school, and the chance to repair their relationship, which had already been edgy to begin with, was running out.

"I'm not sure if I did the right thing or not. What if Oliver's mad at me?"

Taking in all the details of Jennifer's dilemma like a psychiatrist, Granny's wisdom came to the rescue when she said, "Other than provoking him, you handled it well by listening and letting him talk it out. I think that's what he needed all this time."

"But why is he avoiding me now? He hasn't said a word to me since then."

"Oliver's probably just a little confused by everything. That was a pretty big feat—telling you how he felt and what happened to him. What you're not considering here is that he chose you to confess his emotions to. It's obvious he is beginning to trust you."

"Well, he sure saddled me with a lot. I was tongue tied! I couldn't do anything for him, which is basically what he told me. Maybe I should back off and leave him alone."

"For now, it would be a good idea. Give him space to sort himself out."

Jennifer meditated on what Granny said, meanwhile checking her backpack for any items she might have forgotten. Going back to school after summer break was not the time to get caught unprepared. Something as simple as not bringing pencils or notepads would be a first-class ticket to a world of disaster. Inexplicably, Jennifer kept feeling as if she were forgetting one last thing of upmost importance. What was it?

Finally it dawned on her. *My bicycle! Oh no, I didn't air up the tires yet!*

Since the kid prison was somewhat close, she used her bicycle to get there rather than using the school bus.

The popular yellow box on wheels was a no-man's land. All the kids that didn't want to go to school churned within it like angry wasps in a disturbed nest. The whole balance of order was brittle and always on the verge of being set aflame. So at all costs, flat tires or not, Jennifer was not going to resort to using the bus. Today she'd just have to tough it out and walk. At least she and Granny didn't live in the middle of nowhere.

"Do you think Oliver will be OK?" Jennifer asked Granny as she tried to figure out if there was any way around walking to school. Going all that distance on foot seemed daunting, and although she could've asked her grandmother for a ride, she didn't want to endure a lecture for neglecting to add air to her bicycle's tires.

Granny nodded confidently, and before ushering Jennifer out the door, reassured her by saying, "Don't worry about a thing. I'll take care of him."

"How? What are you going to do?"

"Nothing really. Now go on; don't be late for school."

Jennifer clutched the doorframe to keep from being herded out and eyed Granny suspiciously. When she got shooed again, she finally relented and left the house and her defenseless cousin behind.

What is she up to? Jennifer hated it when her grandmother was being secretive, planning something behind her back. Hopefully Oliver wouldn't be in too much trouble while she was gone. But then again, why was she even worrying about it? In fact, she herself was much more unpredictable than Granny. Surely Oliver would be able to handle whatever was up that old lady's sleeve. He'd had plenty of practice anyway.

Comforted by this thought, Jennifer straightened up, squared her shoulders, and set off marching down the road she had lived on for the majority of her life. All the trees that stood proudly along the road seemed to wave in greeting as the soft breeze ruffled their leaves. The crunch of pebbles skittering underneath Jennifer's shoes made her smile; it reminded her of all the times she had traveled down the isolated road, whether skipping along on foot or racing down it on her trusty bicycle.

Her favorite memory was of going to town and slipping into the ancient ice-cream parlor that stood like a monument on the street corner. It really had the best shakes. Granny especially loved it, always stating that they "don't make ice cream like that anymore."

Perhaps next weekend would be a good opportunity to drag Oliver down there and give him a taste of good ole country-style ice cream. City ice cream must be so different, produced from the overused freezers of fast-food stops. Jennifer shuddered. That poor kid was missing out on something incredible! Well, she wasn't going to let that continue any longer. Feeling optimistic again, she picked up the pace and happily kicked stones and leaves, along with unfortunate bugs, out of her path.

Today was going to be a beautiful day, and nothing was going to get in the way of it.

⊨+ +⊨

A quick glance out the window confirmed Oliver's dreaded assumption when he saw Jennifer stomping down the street and kicking rocks into the air like a tornado. She was upset. Why did he have that meltdown? Now he had hurt her feelings and created a huge mess of things. Jennifer never deserved getting the brunt of his frustrations. Nor did he have any right to be rude to her annoying friend that day. Keeping his distance probably wasn't making things any better either. But what was he going to do? He could barely show his face after making such a fool of himself.

Something touched Oliver's shoulder. He looked and saw a wrinkly hand, calloused from years of hard work and in desperate need of a trip to the salon for a massive restoration. Naturally, it was enough to make him jump with fright.

Chuckling, Granny settled him down. "It's only me."

"Uh, OK?" *What does she want?*

"Anyhow, I need your help around the house and in the barn."

"You can't be serious." Oliver had no desire to do chores. He had never done them in the past, and he

139

wasn't about to start now. No way! All he wanted to do was slink into his room and smother his misery with music. From the looks of it, things were about to get a lot worse.

"I'm very serious. Just because I gave you a break this semester doesn't mean you can slack off."

I'll slack when I want. "I shouldn't have to do chores," Oliver grumbled.

"Oh, you wouldn't want an old lady like me to have to do all the work by myself, would you?" Mustering up the most pitiful expression she could, Granny put on a sad face. Creases in her face shifted and exaggerated her frown. She appeared frailer and older than usual.

Old-lady guilt trip, perfectly orchestrated. *Dang, she's good.*

Granny didn't wait for Oliver to think of any excuses. "Good boy, I knew I could rely on you," she said, patting him on the head.

CHAPTER TWENTY-FOUR

The hours crawled by slowly as Oliver worked outside, constantly hounded by Granny, who had an endless list of things to do. The merciless old lady simply stayed on his tail, overseeing how well he did with each task. She had him redo the work whenever he tried to take shortcuts.

It wasn't easy work either. The chores were grueling and backbreaking. Oliver started out by feeding the horses and mucking their stalls, and then he moved on to stacking hay bales in the loft. Afterward he swept the aisle and dusted the rafters, which proved to be an unpleasant job. He inhaled more mold and cobwebs than he could count. The worst part of everything was that *he* was the one doing all the work, while Granny watched closely from her seat on a rickety wooden stool and held a tall glass of refreshing lemonade. The cool ice cubes floated in the drink as she sipped on it. It was unclear whether or not she was trying to taunt Oliver, but it was annoying in so many ways.

"You're doing good; keep it up," Granny said enthusiastically. Her spectacles jiggled as she laughed at Oliver, who glared over the fifty-pound bag of feed he was carrying. Salty sweat dripped from his brow and into his eyes. It burned.

Squinting his eyes in agony, Oliver hobbled down the barn aisle and dropped the heavy bag by the ladder that led up to the loft. Using his shirtsleeve to wipe his face, he glanced up in despair.

How am I going to get this to the loft?

As if reading his mind, Granny said, "I can haul two bags at a time up that ladder any day. I sincerely hope that you're strong enough."

Irritated by the remark, Oliver scooped up the bag of feed and started climbing. Halfway up though, he started to flounder under the weight.

"Huh, I guess my grandson is a weakling."

Evil grandmother! Oliver gritted his teeth and shoved with all his might, pushing the bag over the rungs of the ladder. His bad leg screamed in protest, threatening to buckle. The muscles in his arms strained, and bulging veins rose to the surface. Sweat poured down Oliver's aching back, making his shirt stick to his skin.

With one last hard push, he made it to the loft and sat down, taking a short breather. Only four more bags to go.

⚊⫶ ⫶⚊

Jennifer arrived home to an empty house when she came back from school. Even Creature wasn't anywhere to be seen. It didn't take long to figure out where everyone was; she could hear the low rumbling of a lawn mower outside. Wait, wasn't that her job? She was the one who mowed the grass every so often. Whatever was going on, it definitely had something to do with Granny's last words.

Sure enough, Oliver was puttering around with a push mower and had managed to finish off most of the area around the barn and behind the house. Obviously Granny was trying to teach him some kind of lesson in hard work or something, because they had a perfectly good riding mower stowed in the storage shed. Suddenly, the tired push mower emitted a groaning noise and died on the spot. Thinking it was all a game, Creature ran circles around Oliver and yapped incessantly while he tried to figure out what had just happened.

Granny, who was sitting in the shade of the barn's entrance, waved happily when she saw Jennifer. "Hey, you're home! Did you have a good day?"

"Yeah, it was great! I don't know about him though," Jennifer said, gesturing to Oliver, who was still fighting with the mower. The old rusted pile of metal refused to be brought back to life and gasped each time he yanked on the cord to restart it.

"Oh, he's plenty fine. I'm having him do a little work around the place."

Just now noticing Jennifer, Oliver threw her a desperate look that pleaded for rescue.

"He doesn't seem fine to me."

"Don't worry. I assure you that he's doing well and, I might add, enjoying the time outside. The weather is so beautiful today."

Jennifer didn't know whether Granny was being sarcastic or was completely delusional about the pathetic appearance of her worn-out cousin. She had to help the poor city kid. He was suffering from all this hard work he wasn't used to.

"Um, is it OK if he helps me with my homework?"

Granny thought for a moment, then nodded her approval. "Of course. Go ahead, Oliver. Thanks for helping today."

Oliver seemed genuinely relieved and didn't hesitate to leave the deceased mower behind. Quickly striding up to Jennifer, he grinned excitedly. This was the happiest she had ever seen him.

"Just this once," Jennifer mouthed. Oliver gave a thumbs-up to show that he understood and dashed into the house with Creature chasing after him.

CHAPTER TWENTY-FIVE

O ver the next couple of weeks, Granny stuck to the routine of having Oliver work outside. She made him start early every morning and wouldn't let him off the hook until three in the afternoon. He infinitely despised this new schedule. However, the work eventually got easier as he began to gain strength and bulk up. The one thing he did enjoy was being around the horses and bonding with Jasper, who consumed any treats Oliver fed him. The horse proved to be reliable company whenever Oliver was feeling lonely; Jasper gave him a comforting sense of stability he hadn't had since the accident.

Sometimes Jennifer would snatch Oliver out of Granny's hands on the condition that he helped her with homework. Although he would usually slither away and hide, not bothering to follow through with the so-called condition. After the fifth time of pulling the disappearing act, Jennifer stopped bailing him out.

"Sorry, bud, you've violated your parole too many times," she had said.

Oliver was hopelessly stuck then, and he had to grin and bear the sweat, painful blisters, and simmering heat from the sun. Just when he thought he couldn't stand it anymore, Granny surprised him one weekend by saying he could either work or take a riding lesson. Of course he gladly accepted the offer to ride.

Granny was much better at teaching and explaining things than Jennifer. Granny was nowhere near as insane and was extremely patient. If Oliver messed up on the horse, she simply instructed him to try again. In just one ride, he learned how to steer the horse and ask for different gaits without error. Jasper was the perfect horse to learn on too, because although he was by no means an Olympic jumper, he was very reliable and forgiving when his rider flubbed up. Instead of throwing a fit like Jennifer's horse, Jasper would just respond to the fumbling aids the best he could. It was such a wonderful feeling to be able to accomplish something for once. Riding was as satisfying as running track, if not more. Oliver hungered for another ride, so the next day he asked if they could do a lesson after he did his chores.

Shockingly, Granny not only agreed to give him a lesson, but she also said that he no longer had to work if he rode every day. That's when it finally occurred to him why he was being given stuff to do; Granny was only trying to keep him busy so there was no time to mope anymore. Her method had actually worked without him even realizing it. The dark hole of depression had gone away, and he was somewhat less discontented. For once, he felt good inside.

From that point on, Oliver volunteered to help around the farm and put a lot of effort into his riding in an attempt to get better at it. He didn't want to go back to feeling miserable again. The best part was seeing the joy in Granny's face. She seemed especially pleased when Oliver started learning how to jump.

"Keep yourself steady in the saddle," Granny reminded Oliver as he pointed his mount toward a hurdle. Its poles were set up like an *X*. Jasper popped over it with ease and landed on the other side. Oliver bobbled though and had to rebalance himself.

"Try again."

Oliver steered Jasper in the direction of the hurdle again. This time he managed to keep both feet securely planted in the stirrups and leaned forward slightly, stretching his hands across the horse's neck as they went over. *Perfect.* Oliver gave Jasper a vigorous patting before going up to the arena fence, where Granny was coaching from.

"How'd I do?"

"You did excellently," Granny murmured wistfully.

"What is it? Is everything OK?"

"Oh, it's fine. It's just that when you ride, you remind me so much of…" Granny trailed off. The corners of her lips lifted into a nostalgic smile.

"My dad," Oliver finished for her. It didn't take a genius to know what she was going to say.

"He looked exactly like you when he was your age. I taught him how to ride when he first started. Daniel really had a gift for riding. At the rate you're learning, I think you have the same knack for it."

Whoa, that's kind of deep. "What happened to him? Why did he quit riding?" This question had been bugging Oliver for a long while, so he thought he'd ask up front.

Granny shook her head, saying, "It's a long story, which I'll have to tell some other time. But for now I want to commend you on your hard work lately. You're doing a really good job. Keep it up, and maybe we can think about competing."

Competing—oh, how Oliver missed it. He was competitive by nature, and the urge to win boiled in his blood. The pure joy of having adrenaline powering him on as he pushed himself to do the impossible was like a drug to him. He couldn't live without having some kind of goal or milestone to pass. Without it, his self-esteem literally started to wither into nothingness. He needed to be given challenges that he could achieve and things to look forward to and keep his mind occupied, especially now.

CHAPTER TWENTY-SIX

Watching through the kitchen window while preparing lunch for herself, Jennifer observed her cousin riding in the arena on Jasper. It seemed as if they were having a good time out there. She was taken aback by the progress Oliver was making with his riding. He was already jumping! It certainly wouldn't be long before he'd be as good as she was, which was sort of scary. It had taken ages for Jennifer to get to the point she was at now. Oliver's attitude had also taken a sharp turn. He wasn't as uptight and was optimistic for a change. Whatever Granny was doing, it was helping quite a bit.

Jennifer was just about to start eating when Oliver burst through the back door and swaggered into the kitchen. Even his appearance was different; the sun had faded his hair to a light-wheat color, leaving behind streaky lowlights that looked like strips of spun gold. Defined muscles filled out his tanned arms. His previously listless demeanor was now replaced with a sort of buoyancy, and his walk, although still hindered by a limp, was a bit more energetic. Overall he was a completely different person compared to when he'd first arrived.

"Did you have a good ride?"

"Yeah! I think I'm finally getting the hang of it."

Is he actually smiling? Jennifer had to look twice. "That's great to hear! You know, there's a horse show coming up soon, which I'll be riding in. Maybe you could come and watch."

"That'd be fantastic. It would be cool to see you ride." Oliver sat down gingerly at the table, trying not to agitate his bum leg, which was obviously getting stressed from working. His ear-to-ear grin didn't falter though. How had he gotten to be such a trooper?

Granny's brainwashed him, Jennifer secretly thought, as her grandmother came into the kitchen.

"Well, kids, I just got a call from your uncle. He's coming over this afternoon."

Oh joy. Uncle Stanley's visits were so mundane. The most interesting subject he could talk about was fertilizer. Once a month, he would come to pick up the manure from the farm and carry it off in his truck. In return, Granny would always get part of the earnings that Uncle Stanley made. It was still a mystery what he did with the stuff. The most Jennifer could figure out was that he used it for his miniscule crops or sold it to neighbors. Anyhow, she never cared enough to ask about it.

Fearing she would die from boredom, Jennifer decided to ask Oliver if he would like to go into town for a bit. Surely he found their uncle just as uninteresting as she did. Besides, this would be a good opportunity to have him try some of that special old-fashioned ice cream. It was no surprise though that when she stopped daydreaming and looked up, her cousin had predictably disappeared again. Not everything about him had changed.

⚔ ⚔

Upon receiving the news that drab Uncle Stanley was on his way to spread his dullness around, Oliver retreated to the barn and occupied himself by reading his father's journal. Occasionally he would flip through it for entertainment. If there was any explanation for why his riding had been improving so much, it was probably thanks to the old journal. The pages were chock full of random facts and tips. Each piece of knowledge that Oliver acquired instilled more confidence in him. He was particularly engrossed with the idea of participating in the upcoming competition, although it seemed a little too far-fetched to even hope he could be prepared in time.

"I wonder if I could," Oliver said aloud. No dream was too big, in his opinion.

"Could what?" Walking down the barn aisle, Jennifer came toward Oliver, who was seated on Granny's faithful wooden stool. She noticed the journal in his hands almost immediately. "Oh, were you reading?"

Oops, that was supposed to be a secret. Snapping the journal shut, Oliver nodded hesitantly. "Yeah, I'm not exactly interested in hanging out with Uncle Stanley," he admitted.

"You're not the only one. Our uncle is old school."

"Wow, I guess we both can agree on that!"

"Say, would you like to blow this place and go into town? There's a cool spot I'd like to show you."

"I'm not sure. How are we going to get there? I don't think Gran and Uncle Stanley are going to drive us if they're visiting."

Jennifer shrugged as if it was no big deal. "This isn't the giant city like where you used to live. We can just ride our bikes. Don't worry about it." She beckoned Oliver to follow her. "C'mon out with me to the front yard."

Huh, I'm not convinced. Oliver wasn't sure about going off on some escapade, but the yearning to get out of the house won him over. So he let Jennifer lead him to the front of the house.

Parked in the driveway were two bicycles. One was a bright-orange, reddish color that matched Jennifer's hair. Oliver guessed it belonged to her. The other bicycle was pretty beat up. Most of its black paint was scratched and rubbed off, so it appeared to be peppered with silver. The handlebars were crooked from being bent and then straightened back out so many times, probably due to a reckless kid trashing it on a daily basis. Even the front wheel was slightly tilted to the right.

"That one's yours. Granny and I got it from a garage sale a week before you came. Figured you could use a bike," Jennifer said, pointing to the old pile of rust. "Don't worry; we'll find a better one for you sooner or later. I know it's a piece of junk, isn't it?"

"I suppose so." Oliver smiled sheepishly. He didn't want to say outright that he thought it was the ugliest, junkiest bike he'd ever seen.

CHAPTER TWENTY-SEVEN

On the outskirts of the town where Jennifer and Oliver came in, there was a vast array of ancient houses. Weather-beaten picket fences bordered the properties. Every now and then, a dog would suddenly wake up and start barking from its yard as Jennifer and Oliver sped past on their bicycles. The farther they traveled, the more modern the houses were. Eventually they made it past the neighborhood and kept going until they reached a main street that led to a touristy town where multiple antique shops, old pubs, and restaurants were set up.

The place was picturesque; neatly trimmed trees shaded the brick cobblestone sidewalks, which were occupied by ambling people dressed in summery clothes and flip-flops, including shades and stylish hats. Large shopping bags swung from just about everyone's hands. Vibrant flowers dotted the scene with shades of red, orange, and yellow. Slick black lampposts stood regally on each corner. Tired shoppers slouched on cast-iron benches and sipped on their cool drinks to refresh themselves.

Oliver was in awe of everything. He had assumed he was in the middle of nowhere, miles away from civilization, but he had been dead wrong. This town was a breath of fresh air for him, and he could already see himself hanging around here in the future, perhaps with some new friends too.

Going all the way to the end of the street, Jennifer stopped in front of one of the stores and hopped off her bicycle. After parking it, she rushed inside. Oliver did the same but took the time to glance up at the neon sign above the door, which read

Mercury's Ice-Cream Shoppe.

Interesting, Oliver thought as he stepped in and looked around for his cousin. The atmosphere of the ice-cream parlor was retro and looked as if it was from another dimension in time—trapped in the 80s. Metallic stools resided by the long bar, and funky lights hung from the ceiling. A jukebox sat in the corner, erupting with Cyndi Lauper music. Light poured in through the large windows and lit up the crowded booths. Jennifer was already seated in one next to a window.

Making eye contact, she smiled and waved. Oliver strode across the black-and-white checkered tile floor to join her. As soon as he slid into the booth, she tossed a menu at him.

"Go on; make an order!" she said.

Picking up the menu, Oliver skimmed through it and analyzed the kooky stuff it offered up. In the end, he settled on a banana split. He wasn't in an adventurous mood right now. Jennifer was less than pleased with his choice, though, and taunted him.

"A banana split? I take you all the way here and you order a banana split? How boring can you be?"

"Hey, I like banana splits! Let me pick what I want. Anyway, what are you ordering?"

"I'm getting a Coke float," Jennifer boasted.

"What in the world is that?"

"It's Coca-Cola with vanilla ice cream."

Oliver's face twisted at the revolting description. "That's disgusting."

"They have all kinds of other flavors though. I recommend Orange Crush."

"Still disgusting. I'm going to pass, thanks."

"Coward." Jennifer smirked and was going to throw out another witty comment when a cheery waitress appeared by the table. The diversion gave Oliver a chance to study his surroundings again. All his life, he had always wanted to know what was going on around him, almost to the point that it was a necessity.

As he scanned the people in the restaurant and observed them, he began to get a sense of being watched. Soon enough, he noticed the scrutinizing glare being directed at him. A guy around his age was comfortably situated in one of the booths between two attractive girls. The pair of eyes were penetratingly dark as they stared, much like two black coals simmering in a fireplace.

Why is he looking at me like that? Oliver thought, twitching nervously.

"Oliver! She's waiting for your order."

"Huh?" With a jolt, he turned his attention to Jennifer and the waitress, who were both looking at him impatiently. Listening wasn't exactly his strong point. "Erm…banana split."

The waitress gave a forced smile that said, *finally*, and scribbled the order onto the piece of paper she was holding. Then she turned on her heel and sped off to assist the other diners that had been delayed.

"Where's your head, city boy?" Jennifer rolled her eyes and pushed a glass of water toward him. "There's your drink. I wasn't sure what you wanted, so I didn't ask for anything special."

When did the waitress bring drinks to the table? Plain water wasn't that savory either. Served him right, though, for zoning out. Oliver said thanks anyway and took the glass. Curious about the situation with the peculiar guy earlier, he glanced in that direction again.

The guy was no longer staring, having returned to chatting with his friends. They all flocked around him as if he were a messiah. One of the girls sitting next to him seemed overly giddy when the hotshot casually draped an arm around her shoulders.

Something pelted the side of Oliver's head. He ducked in time to avoid getting hit by the next round of wadded paper mini balls.

What the heck?

Holding a straw, Jennifer blew on it like a smoking pistol, then proceeded to reload with more ammunition. Oliver snatched the straw from her before she could shoot more paper balls at him.

"Hey, give it back!"

"No."

"Spoilsport," Jennifer said huffily. "So, what's bothering you?"

Did she read my mind? "Nothing's bothering me. What are you talking about?"

"You're lying."

"I'm not." *Liar, liar, pants on fire.*

"Yeah, you are. You've got that look on your face again."

"What look?"

Jennifer chuckled and demonstrated by craning her neck and putting on an expression that was a combination of nervousness and bemusement. "You space out, and your eyes glaze over like you're turning into a zombie."

"I don't act like that."

"You also start mumbling and fidgeting with whatever's in your hands."

"Jeez, am I like your research project or something? How do you come up with those facts?" Oliver looked down and realized he had twisted the straw he'd stolen earlier into a million knots. Oops, Jennifer wasn't kidding.

"All right, you got me," he admitted and gestured to the gawker, who was now chowing down on an exceptionally large sundae. "Do you know who that guy is?"

Jennifer didn't even bother to look. "That would be Jason Watts Jr., the most popular Casanova in high school. He's the notorious playboy of the town and a renowned highflier in the horse-show jumping circuit."

"Whoa, he must be a cool kid."

"Nah, he's not worth squat. Jason's a real jerk to anyone who doesn't bow down to him. He was sizing you up earlier, if you're wondering why he was staring. You're the new kid on *his* turf."

"I guess he's bad news then."

"You don't want anything to do with him. Anyway, here comes our food!" The subject was quickly dropped when the peppy waitress came back and placed the banana split and the Coke float in front of Jennifer and Oliver. After smiling and telling them to enjoy their food, she skipped off again.

The banana split was a beauty to behold: three perfectly round scoops of chocolate, vanilla, and strawberry ice cream sat parallel to a fresh banana. A generous serving of chocolate syrup was drizzled on top. Taking a spoon, Oliver took a bite. It was almost a shame to mutilate the piece of art.

"I'm in heaven," he murmured blissfully as the cold, ridiculously sweet goodness melted in his mouth. It was one of the best things he had ever tasted in his life. What had he been missing out on all this time?

CHAPTER TWENTY-EIGHT

Oliver thought back to the strange conversation he had stumbled on when he got back home from the little field trip Jennifer had taken him on. He was about to open the front door when he heard Granny and Uncle Stanley standing on the other side and talking. Pressing his ear to the rough wood covered with chipped paint, he listened in. But not without a struggle—the words dribbled through with about as much ease as sifting rocks through mesh. Only a minority of the conversation managed to get past the door.

"He's been...really well lately," Granny had said. "Think...horses...helping a lot."

Uncle Stanley was even harder to understand, since he always mumbled. "Did...about his..."

"No…haven't explained…father yet. Maybe…other time."

Uncle Stanley mumbled something in agreement, and then the door knob started to turn. Moving fast, Oliver ducked out of sight so they wouldn't catch him eavesdropping. From around the corner of the house, he watched as his uncle slowly meandered down to his truck, got in, and drove off into the encroaching darkness of dusk. As perplexing as the conversation was, Oliver didn't quite have the guts to ask Granny or Jennifer about it, fearing that whatever they were talking about would be bad. It couldn't have been anything good. Why else would Granny be hesitant to talk about his father; had he done something wrong?

Oliver didn't really want to find out. It had already been a week since overhearing parts of Granny and Uncle Stanley's conversation, and he was doing just fine without knowing. Like the saying went, what he didn't know wouldn't hurt him. Besides, if he was going have any hope of riding in the Autumn Kellert Show, there was no time to waste being distracted by other things. He had to make every minute count. So the next morning, he put his worries to the side and focused on getting Jasper tacked up and ready to ride. He had a lesson soon.

This time, however, Granny wasn't going to be the one teaching. To everyone's delight, Annamarie volunteered to take on teaching and help Oliver be ready in time for the competition. This was a dream come true for him right now, knowing he had a good shot at accomplishing a goal and maybe even winning. There was more involved than just entering the competition. It was also about proving to himself that he could move on and be good at something other than running track. Ultimately, competing was proof he could find joy again and that marching forward in life was actually worth the effort.

It was a day like any other day in school—boring and a waste of time and sanity. That is, until Jason Watts Jr. decided to corner Jennifer in the hall right before the last class. Everything just got that much worse.

"Hello, Jen. How's that nutty horse of yours doing?" His ugly sneer spelled trouble. It was ironic, though, that even his sneer couldn't demolish his good looks. He always came out on top, no matter what.

"Get lost, Junior," Jennifer snapped, knowing he absolutely hated being called that. They had known each other since kindergarten. Instead of friendship, hatred had festered between them as they grew up. "I've got to go."

Jason flinched but quickly shrugged off the insult and brushed back his shiny jet-black hair that was swept to the side so perfectly that it looked sculpted. "You can go, but you might be missing out on a chance to persuade me not to spread rumors," he said, taunting her.

You've got to be kidding me. "What rumors?"

"Hmm, something to do with your cousin."

"Such as?"

"His parents are dead, so he's living with you and your grandmother. And he's a deaf, crippled has-been. I really wonder how he's going to fare in the competition."

"How'd you find this out?"

"Oh, did you think I didn't notice you two at Mercury's?" he asked with a dark chuckle. "I just asked your loyal friend Lyndsey about your cousin, and she spilled everything. She's such a sap. Anyway, all I had to do was look up Oliver's name, and I found out even more."

Jennifer bristled at the insidious remarks. "I don't have time for this."

Ignoring her, Jason put a finger on his angular jaw as if he were contemplating. "Of course, you wouldn't know that your cousin used to be most popular guy in his old school. Hope he's not expecting that to continue here." Jason suddenly narrowed his eyes. A vicious gleam sparked in them. "Everyone's going to just love him when they learn about his father."

"Leave him alone. He doesn't deserve any more misery," Jennifer warned. "What is it that you want?"

"Keep him out of the competitions."

"What? No! He's been practicing for months."

"Exactly. I want to win."

"Oh, come on. He's not even going to be in your class. What's the big deal?"

"You sure are dim, aren't you? Just think about it…if anybody gets wind that he's the 'famous' Daniel Murray's son, the horse community is going to be all over him. I don't plan to share the spotlight with that underdog."

"But—"

"Tell him to give up the idea of competing, and I will leave him alone. Simple as that."

Jennifer faltered, unsure what to say in return. Oliver would be severely upset both ways, and there was nothing she could do to protect him from Jason's threats. She needed to think this over.

"I see you're not really convinced." Jason sneered again. "How's this: I'll ruin *your* reputation if you don't get rid of that deadbeat."

"Fine! I'll work something out." Jennifer realized this situation was only going to get worse if she stuck around, so she pushed past Jason and rushed to class, which was already starting. After a quick apology to the displeased teacher, she hunkered down in her chair and tried to listen, but she couldn't concentrate. What was she going to do? This was turning out to be one huge mess, and she was about be caught right in the middle of it. God, she hated Jason. He was such a monster!

She knew one thing for certain though. She wasn't going to give in to his phony threats. What could he really do? He was always full of baloney anyway. With that in mind, she was able to put her worries to rest, for now at least.

Jennifer finally got home after a long, miserable day. She was ragged and tired. All the worries swirling in her mind were taking a toll. Creature brightened her mood a little when he greeted her at the door. He was getting pretty big now, almost full grown. Jennifer gave the dog a quick cuddle and headed straight for the barn, seeking to find some comfort from her horse Pompeii. If anything could cheer her up, it was being in the barn.

Oliver was out in the arena; he had just finished riding and was cooling off Jasper. He looked rather chuffed too. Clearly his first riding lesson with Annamarie had gone really well. His naturally reserved smile, which always tended to be somewhat lopsided, grew bigger when he saw Jennifer walking up.

"Hi!" Oliver greeted her, still a person of few words.

"Hey there!" Jennifer tried to sound cheerful, but it was a hard challenge considering her mood. "Did ya have a good ride?"

Bubbly Annamarie nodded enthusiastically and butted in, answering before Oliver could say anything. "He's a real sport; he never gives up and keeps on trying again and again. I didn't expect him to be such a determined rider. The lesson went beautifully!"

Oliver blushed under the praise. "I'm not *that* good."

"Don't be so modest. You were great! I have to say that you definitely have a knack for riding."

A twinge of jealousy jabbed at Jennifer. She knew she should be happy for Oliver, but hearing Annamarie say he was a good rider was annoying nevertheless. She never got compliments so freely from Annamarie, who had been her coach for years.

Shake it off. He's only having beginner's luck.

"Oh, I just remembered something," Annamarie piped up again, smiling as if she had something up her sleeve.

"What?" *Hmm, maybe she's spared some praise for me after all. Good grief, I was feeling down for no reason.*

"If it's OK with you, I'd like to switch out your lesson and teach Oliver tomorrow since we're pressed for preparation time."

"Uh…" Jennifer was flabbergasted. What about her? She was competing too! This wasn't fair in the least bit, being asked to forfeit her riding lesson tomorrow. As much as she wanted to protest and complain, she solemnly nodded in fake approval.

"Thanks, Jennifer. You're very sweet and understanding. I'm confident that you're capable of getting ready for the competition on your own. Oliver needs all the help he can get right now."

"No problem." But Jennifer didn't understand. Not in the least. This was an abomination!

CHAPTER TWENTY-NINE

The gray horse tossed his head for the thousandth time as Jennifer brought him around to the oxer that she had been attempting to jump for the last ten minutes. Like an array of little clouds, gobs of frothy white sweat splotched Pompeii's tense neck. His bulging black eyes rolled. He took rigid strides as he cantered toward the ominous oxer.

Jennifer dug in with her spurs and pushed the resilient horse forward. She blocked the horse from darting to the left with her outside rein. This time, though, Pompeii ran out to the right at the last moment and skidded past the oxer. He tossed his head again, flinging flecks of foam in the air.

"Ugh!" Jennifer exclaimed in frustration. Her cheeks were as red as her hair, which stuck out from underneath the riding helmet like rogue flames.

"Do you want me to lower the poles?" Oliver offered. He shifted to rebalance himself on his perch. He had been sitting on the arena fence and watching Jennifer and her horse fuss at each other for a quite a while. Pompeii was not willing to work today. Every chance he got, he threw his head up and down, crow-hopped, and refused to jump anything that was any taller than a foot.

The absence of Annamarie's assistance during today's ride wasn't doing Jennifer any favors. Annamarie had arrived early in the morning to teach Oliver and had taken off long before Jennifer had gotten back home from school. Presumably she guessed that Jennifer was less than pleased with her and wanted to avoid confrontation. Smart choice, Oliver figured.

Likewise, Jennifer was in no mood to deal with her horse's antics. She popped the reins when Pompeii started to jig. For some reason, she was ready to spit acid at any given moment. Oliver knew to keep a low profile and let her work out whatever was wrong.

"No, that's OK. I'm just going to go over the cross-rails and end this ride on a somewhat good note."

Taking a deep breath, Jennifer kicked Pompeii into a canter and steered him toward a small green-and-white-striped *X* that sat in the corner of the arena. The horse eyed the hurdle as they approached.

Jennifer smacked him with her crop for good measure. With a defiant snort, Pompeii charged over the jump and then bolted after landing. Jennifer wrestled the horse back down to a walk again and gave him a pat on the neck. It wasn't a very good pat though. It was more of a slap. It was fairly obvious that Jennifer was pretty annoyed.

"OK, I think we're done for today."

"I'm sorry you had such a rough ride," Oliver said.

"What are you apologizing for? It's not your fault that Pompeii was being a blockhead."

"Well, I feel bad about the switch of the lesson times. I shouldn't have let that happen. It's not fair that you had to give up your lesson for me."

Jennifer rolled her eyes exasperatedly and dismounted from Pompeii. Then she whisked off her helmet and let her hair loose. Because of the heat and sweat, it remained frizzy and wild.

"Don't worry about it. Annamarie made the decision, not us," she said, reassuring him. Her words came out bluntly though, and she didn't seem to want to talk anymore. Giving a sharp yank on the reins, she marched off. Pompeii scrambled to keep from being dragged along. Just before getting out of earshot, Jennifer glanced over her shoulder at Oliver. "Don't forget that we have to leave soon!" she hollered.

"Leave for where?"

"The tack store!"

Oh, right. Oliver had almost forgotten about the plan to make a trip to the tack store. He was in dire need of some riding gear. Jeans and tennis shoes were not very ideal for show jumping, and especially not for competing. Plus, he needed a new helmet to wear. The hand-me-down one from Jennifer didn't fit well, and Granny was getting more preoccupied by the day that he would get hurt if he fell off. It was fair enough to be concerned. The helmet was way too small, and it left a worrisome amount of uncovered area on his head.

Jennifer usually joked that Oliver's thick, shaggy hair would provide ample cushion, but that was back when she hadn't been in such a touchy mood. Maybe the trip to the tack store would cheer her up. He could only hope.

There were so many pairs of riding breeches hanging on racks that they created a sea of fabric, flustering Jennifer to no end. She and Granny had scoped out nearly the whole selection with minimal success. As luck would have it, Oliver was maddeningly difficult to fit because his legs were long and he had a skinny waistline. All the breeches kept winding up too short. When they tried a size larger, the pants would be too big around his waist. His pickiness made it all the worse. He complained and shunned just about everything.

The Equestrian Shop had a vast variety of horse and riding gear and supplies, but nothing could satisfy Oliver when it came to clothes. By this point, Jennifer was ready to throw up her hands and call it quits. Granny kept searching though, determined to find something that would work.

So far they had found shirts, riding gloves, and even a striking pair of boots. But they still lacked the most challenging item of all—breeches—which was the one accessory of riding attire that had a despicable reputation of being uncomfortable and rarely fitting well.

"Aha!" Granny somehow found riding breeches that Oliver hadn't tried on yet. Ripping them from the rack in triumph, she handed them to Jennifer. "See if he likes these."

Jennifer graciously took them and stroked the ebony fabric. The belt loops and pockets were even lined with decorative stitching. The breeches were definitely quality, perhaps the best pair in the store. A glimpse of the daunting price tag confirmed they were certainly the most expensive. Oliver had to like this pair. Surely he would.

Walking up to the dressing room, Jennifer pounded on the door and announced that she had another pair of riding breeches for him to try on. There was a small shuffle inside. Seconds later the door cracked open, and a hand darted out and snatched the breeches from Jennifer. Then the hand quickly pulled the door shut again with the same efficient speed as a trap-door spider.

Jennifer couldn't help but chuckle at her cousin's goofiness. He was odd in so many ways. She doubted she would ever truly figure him out. Nevertheless, he was entertaining sometimes. While Oliver dillydallied about in the dressing room, Jennifer mustered up the dregs of her dwindling patience and waited. Finally Oliver came out with the breeches on. He walked awkwardly, as if his legs were made of wood, and his contorted face expressed his discomfort.

"So, do they fit?" Jennifer asked anyway. She discreetly crossed her fingers behind her back. Maybe there was a chance.

"No."

Ugh! It took a lot of effort for Jennifer to refrain from throwing her hands in the air and screaming bloody murder. "Why? They look great on you!" It was no lie either; the breeches really did look good on Oliver. They were the right length for once and complimented his athletic build.

The same old excuse immediately rattled out. "They're too tight."

"They aren't either! I think they're perfect. You just have to get used to them is all. Breeches are supposed to fit tightly."

Oliver frowned, making it clear that he didn't believe a word Jennifer said. "All these riding pants look like leotards," he complained. "They're so sissy—"

"They're not sissy!" Jennifer interjected. She was tired of listening to her cousin moan about the breeches. "Let's give them a try. We can always return them later."

"I feel exposed in these."

"Now you're being dramatic. Stop it."

"Can't I use normal pants?"

Jennifer shook her head. "Sorry, that won't work." No longer willing to delegate, she grabbed Oliver by the hand and dragged him to a display nearby, which held multiple riding helmets. She quickly picked one out and offered it to him. But as usual her uncooperative cousin balked.

"I don't like the way it looks."

"Too bad," Jennifer said, taking the helmet and cramming it onto Oliver's head. She had to reach up high, since he was taller than she was. His fussing and fidgeting did not make things any easier. When she attempted to adjust the chin strap, he pulled away defiantly.

"I can do it myself!" he grumbled.

"Fine. Go ahead." Sighing, Jennifer backed off and watched as Oliver fumbled in vain, trying to close the strap. His hearing aids squealed in protest at being squashed under the helmet. The noise was loud enough to capture the attention of several other people in the store, who looked at him questioningly.

Boys, they're all the same…always thinking that they know everything.

Oliver eventually got the helmet strapped on, although tufts of his bushy hair pushed past the brim, which kind of ruined the elegance of it. His sulky stature and the intolerant glare in his icy-blue eyes weren't flattering either. The ugly expression worsened when Jennifer asked him to tuck his shirt in and put on the boots he had picked out earlier. Nevertheless, with the riding outfit put together, he managed to look like a model straight out of an equestrian magazine.

Granny clearly thought so too when she came around to see him dressed up. "You look stunning," she gushed. "Very fetching." She had that wistful look again. For whatever reason, she had always seemed to feel affectionate appreciation for Oliver. It was if he were a memento somehow, most likely reminding Granny of his father.

"Can I get out of these clothes?" Oliver moaned, pulling the helmet off. He wasn't fond of playing dress-up. "I'm getting tired."

Jennifer couldn't blame him either, watching as he bickered and fussed under Granny's ogling. Chuckling to herself, Jennifer meandered off and left him to his own devices. There were more interesting things to do than listen to her cousin and grandmother debate over clothes. Jennifer knew how the two of them were; neither one would back down without a long discussion.

It would probably be a while before they came to an agreement.

So while she waited for them to work it out, Jennifer passed the time by browsing through a display of halters. Some were black or brown leather with shiny brass hardware, and there were also multiple nylon ones that came in bright colors. One maroon halter in particular caught her attention, and she picked it up, wondering how it would look on Pompeii. She could just imagine the purplish color contrasting nicely against his handsome gray face.

He could really use a new halter, Jennifer thought. It would certainly be an improvement compared to the old ratty one Pompeii had, which was frayed and exhausted from years of use. But was she really willing to spend half her savings on a new halter? As she stood there, trying to decide, she began to get the icky sense that she wasn't alone. She looked up and scanned the store, eventually spotting an irritatingly familiar person lurking just a few feet away.

Of all people, it was Jason, staring her down in the most unsettling way. His accusatory gaze shifted to Oliver for a moment and then went back to her. The look on his face said it all: *You didn't listen to me. You're in for it big time.*

Jennifer cringed and veered off in the opposite direction. She didn't want to face Jason or have anything to do with him. Fortunately, her cousin and grandmother were just now checking out at the counter. But leaving the store didn't exactly mean she was escaping the brewing storm. The worst part of the whole situation was not knowing what Jason was planning to do, or when his revenge would come.

CHAPTER THIRTY

It was a chilly morning, presenting a dreary start for Thursday, and Oliver felt just as drab as the weather as he went out to the barn. The fact that he had already lived at the farmhouse for over five months now was surreal. He would not have believed it if it hadn't been for the signs of summer coming to an official end. It wasn't as hot anymore; instead, it was cooler in the mornings and afternoons. In addition, the autumn colors of reds, oranges, yellows, and browns had appeared, and a few trees were even starting to drop their leaves.

The horses were indifferent to the essence of changing seasons. For them it was just another morning. The moment they saw him, they started to nicker and stamp their feet in anticipation. They were starving for their breakfast, and thus making their typical melodramatic commotion while Oliver trudged back and forth down the aisle with buckets of feed. Eventually the ruckus died down as he dumped the grain into each horse's food bin, threw down hay, and made sure every stall had buckets of fresh water. He then spent a moment or so giving Jasper extra attention, who was happily munching away on his grain and hay.

Satisfied that everything was in order, he gave the horse a quick pat and went back to the house. Creature was already there to greet him when he opened the door. The dog barked excitedly, then spun around and took off, streaking through the house. Oliver shook his head in annoyance and went to the living room to watch television. The crazy dog, who had tripled in size lately, was becoming a nuisance. At least he kept the house lively. Things were awfully quiet with Jennifer away at school, and Granny had gone to Uncle Stanley's to visit. So it was just Oliver and the animals, home alone with no one else around.

Annamarie wasn't going to be coming over either. Out of the blue yesterday, she had cancelled all the riding lessons, saying that she had received a job offer that she just couldn't turn down. Apparently she had hired on as a full-time trainer for another stable, but in order to take the job, she had to quit teaching Jennifer and Oliver. She didn't have enough time to keep up two jobs at once. Tomorrow she was going to pick up her horse, Valencia, and move her to the other stable she was going to start working at.

Annamarie's announcement that she would no longer be Jennifer and Oliver's trainer was so sudden and unexpected that it threw everyone for a loop. Jennifer was in an absolute tizzy over it; her current mood was about as endearing as that of a crabby badger rooted up from its den. She didn't seem to be mad at Annamarie though. It was almost as if she were blaming someone else for the situation. But who?

Oliver dismissed the complicated thoughts and settled on the living-room couch. Whatever it was that had Jennifer so worked up didn't really involve him. At least he hoped not. He yawned and stretched out, propping his feet up on one armrest and leaning his head back on the other one. Now there was nothing left to do but wait. He glanced at the grandfather clock that was stuffed away in the corner of the living room. The time proclaimed it to be eight thirty. Jennifer would be home before Granny, but it was hours before school would be over. How could he wait that long? It was already boring enough sitting all alone in the empty house.

Sighing, Oliver reached for the TV remote on the coffee table and turned on the television. As usual there was nothing of interest to watch. After flipping through all of the channels twice, he decided to stick with the channel Granny typically watched.

Better than nothing, he thought as he watched some show about seeing big cats on safari. Since he could barely hear the TV, there was no thrill in watching the screen zoom in on a rather large lion who was apparently roaring at the top of his lungs. The lion shook his thick, matted mane and cast one last glare at the camera before sauntering off to be with his pride. Then the camera went back to focusing on the safari guide, who was yammering on about the lions.

Oliver's eyes slowly glazed over as he stared dully at the muffled TV. *This is stupid,* he thought bitterly. Suddenly feeling rebellious, he grabbed the remote off the coffee table and turned the volume up to full blast. It didn't matter how loud it was. Nobody else was home.

Creature, who was sleeping peacefully in the middle of the living-room carpet, was startled awake by the sudden explosion of noise. With his bat-like ears pinned back, the dog looked around with eyes the size of marbles. He didn't plan to stick around. Yipping in protest, he bolted out of the living room. Oliver paid no attention to Creature's antics. Instead he just lay there on the couch and happily absorbed the vibrations and broken sounds that thundered in the room.

I should do this more often, he thought in amusement.

The thud of the front door slamming shut woke him from his slumber. He quickly sat up and blinked in surprise. When did he fall asleep, and how long had he been out? While he rubbed his eyes, he caught a glimpse of Jennifer rushing through the living room with both hands over her ears. Creature came out from nowhere and barked frantically, probably relieved that he was finally going to be rescued.

"For crying out loud, where's the remote?" Jennifer yelled. Her attempts to talk over the television were hopelessly overridden by the noise that boomed throughout the whole house. The noisy environment was a perfect setting for Oliver but most definitely not for Jennifer, nor Lyndsey, who was standing at the doorway.

Aww man, what is she doing here? He still wasn't exactly fond of Lyndsey. She was so obnoxious, in his opinion.

Oliver's attention was diverted when Jennifer found the TV remote and turned off the television, eradicating the glorious noise he constantly craved. "Why'd you turn it off?" he protested. "I was watching that show!"

"Lyndsey and I could hear the racket a whole block away! What in the world are you trying to do, break the TV?" Jennifer scolded. It felt as if her green eyes were boring right through him like two laser beams.

"It wasn't that loud. Why are you making such a big deal out of it?"

"I'm not, Oliver. But you've got to consider others once in a while. Not everyone is deaf like you."

"I know that! You really don't have to point that out."

"Actually, I do. You never pay attention to how much trouble you cause sometimes."

"Trouble? What do you mean—"

"Um, is everything all right?" Lyndsey interrupted the conversation. By now, she had figured it was safe enough to enter the house and was cautiously venturing into the living room. Although she never bothered to acknowledge Oliver. Ever since he had snapped at her that one time, she had been a bit on the aloof side. Apparently she hadn't completely forgiven him yet. Not that he cared though.

Jennifer scoffed. "Sorry; he's just being an idiot again. I don't know what he's trying to achieve here." She cast another glare at Oliver. "C'mon, Lyndsey. Let's go upstairs."

"Hey, wait a moment!" Oliver yelled after the two girls when they started to walk off. They had no right to treat him like that. After all, he hadn't done anything that wrong. "What's your problem? Why are you so upset with me?"

Jennifer stopped and turned around. She looked even more irritated than before. "You're the problem! If it weren't for you, Annamarie wouldn't have quit, and Jason wouldn't be wrecking my life."

"Jason? What does this have to do with him?" Oliver snapped back. "I didn't cause Annamarie to quit. It's not my fault!"

Seeming to be left with nothing else to say, Jennifer threw her hands in the air in defeat. "Ugh, you're impossible; of course Annamarie leaving is your fault. Jason is hassling me because he doesn't want you to compete."

In a huff, she turned and stomped upstairs to her bedroom. A moment later, the sound of the door slamming shut echoed through the house. Lyndsey, on the other hand, stayed behind. With her bottom lip stuck out in a pouty fashion and her arms crossed, she glowered down at Oliver. "You know you should be nicer to her."

"Oh really?" *I think Jennifer could use the same advice.*

"Yeah," said Lyndsey. "She's getting tired of having to put up with you all the time. In fact, she's told me that she wishes you had never moved in. And I don't blame her. Nobody really wants a psyched-out throwaway hanging around, especially not a jerk who's too dumb to appreciate what he *does* have."

"Y...you're lying," Oliver stuttered, taken aback by the unexpected accusations. Why was she saying that? What had he done wrong? "I'm not like that. Besides, Jennifer and I get along just fine."

"No, I'm not lying. Jennifer is only tolerating you being here. She doesn't really like you, nor does her grandmother, who pitied you enough to take you in. I feel entirely the same. You don't belong here. They should've just put you in an orphanage or something and been done with it."

Deciding that she'd gotten her point across, Lyndsey started heading upstairs. Halfway up though, she looked back over her shoulder and remarked, "Keep behaving the way you are, and your grandmother may actually do that!"

Then she disappeared, leaving the hurtful words suspended in the air. Somehow, it felt worse now than when she started telling him off. Perhaps everything she said was finally beginning to sink in. Nevertheless, Oliver was officially alone again. He sighed and buried his face in his hands, wishing he could forget everything Jennifer and Lyndsey said. But the words stuck firmly, imbedded deep in his mind.

Why am I such a mess-up? Oliver wondered. Surely that stuff wasn't true. He wasn't really a psyched-out jerk, was he? Maybe the girls were both spouting off and making it all up. How was he causing trouble, and why would Jason care whether or not he competed in the horse show? He could not figure any of it out. The worst thought of all was losing everything again. If Jennifer and Granny disliked him enough, it was certainly possible that they'd kick him out the first chance they got.

The vision of being ripped away from his new life made Oliver feel vulnerable and unsteady. He wouldn't be able to handle it. Maybe he should listen to Lyndsey and try to be on good behavior for a while. It didn't seem like a bad idea after all.

⊷≺+ +≻⊷

Quietly closing the door behind her, Lyndsey came into the room and sat down on the bed next to Jennifer.

"Are you all right?" Lyndsey asked.

"That was quite a fiasco, wasn't it?" Jennifer asked. She felt kind of embarrassed about the whole show that had taken place downstairs. "I know I'm being really hard on him, but what I said was truthful. Ever since he came, things have been turned upside down. Now to top it off, you just broke the news to me today that you're moving to New York of all places. It was kind of the last straw for me, and I think that's why I snapped at Oliver."

Lyndsey shrugged and said, "I understand what you're saying. If it makes you feel better, I sorted out your cousin and told him that he should be nicer for a change. He shouldn't be giving you any trouble now. And don't worry, my parents and I aren't going to be moving away permanently. It's just for a year."

"Thanks for sticking up for me. But as for moving, a year seems like an awfully long time," Jennifer said, feeling sad that she would have to say goodbye to her friend. Tonight was the last night that Lyndsey would be visiting. It would probably be a long time before they saw each other again in person.

As if reading her mind, Lyndsey smiled and said, "On the bright side, we can Skype each other or text. With the technology these days, we'll have no problem keeping in touch, right?"

That made Jennifer perk up a little. "You have a good point there. It'll be just like when you were in Florida. Be sure to take lots of pictures for me! I wanna know all about what it's like living in the Big Apple."

Lyndsey laughed. "I certainly will!"

CHAPTER THIRTY-ONE

Sitting cross legged on the floor of his bedroom, Oliver's heart kept rising to his throat at the sight of the cardboard box in front of him. After previously refusing to open it, he had finally gathered enough courage to cut the tape that sealed it shut and lift the lid. But it was harder than he predicted, taking the next step of actually looking inside. By this point, it seemed that he'd have better luck convincing himself to thrust his hand in a fire and let it melt off. Did he really want to be reminded of what he had lost? He wasn't so sure. However, he was sure of one thing: hiding out in his room and doing this difficult project was so much easier than having to deal with Jennifer and her friend

Lyndsey, who unfortunately hadn't left yet. They were *still* visiting together, despite it being past ten at night. Girls were weird, to say the least.

Ah heck, just do it, Oliver thought determinedly, reaching into the box.

The first things he pulled out were his track clothes, all neatly folded in a stack. Next were some trophies and posters plus some electronics—his computer, various games, and his phone—which he set aside for later. Eventually he came across some old photos; most of them were of track races. He took his time to analyze them, and he reflected back on the good memories. They made him happy but also a little emotional. As much as he tried to fight the sadness, it shrouded him like a fog.

One photo in particular caught Oliver's attention. It was his favorite shot. His life had been so scrambled that he had completely forgotten about it. With an anxious gulp, he grasped the picture in both hands and stared fervently at his motionless family, who were sealed over with glass and surrounded by a frame.

The picture showed him as a skinny twelve-year-old. Sidled up next to him was his little sister, Emma, who held his hand tightly. Her toothy smile was radiant, like the bright-orange sundress she wore, and she had her blond hair tied back with a big flouncy bow. Oliver's appearance was a bit more conservative in his plain T-shirt and sport shorts. Their parents stood behind them, proudly smiling from ear to ear.

Their mother was just as flamboyantly dressed as Emma, but their father looked more like Oliver, with a recently trimmed goatee, somewhat brushed hair, and comfortable leisure clothes. They were all in a lavish outdoor park. The summer sun shone down on a huge water fountain in the distance. The spray of water glittered as the sunlight captured it, creating prism-like colors to appear on the blue of the cloudless sky. Overall it was a picture that happened to catch a perfect moment on a flawless day full of happiness and sunshine. A memory that was worth holding on to forever. Oliver definitely didn't plan on letting it go.

Still hanging on to the picture, he peered into the box again and noticed there was still one more thing left in the bottom: a worn-out teddy bear literally held together by patches and thread. Its eyes had been replaced with a pair of black buttons, and the russet fur was tattered and thinned out. Its neck especially looked bare and naked without the tied ribbon that it used to wear.

Oliver tenderly picked the teddy bear up, remembering the day he had gone with his mother to the store and helped find toys for Emma when she was born. He had selected the teddy bear himself, thinking she would like it. The old stuffed animal turned out to be her favorite possession. She even named it after Oliver, always calling it Ollie Bear. Besides pictures, it was the only physical thing left of her.

Sighing heavily so that his breath came out in a whoosh, he got up and carried the faithful teddy bear to his bed. Hitting the hay seemed like the easiest way to forget the harsh truth of everything going on around him. Oliver already began to feel slightly better as he covered himself with the warm blankets and sank into the cushiness of his pillow. Once settled, he took the teddy bear and wrapped his arms around it. It seemed like a childish thing to do, snuggling with a stuffed animal at his age, but he didn't care as long as it brought him comfort.

"Come on; just one more time," Oliver said the next day, doing his best to persuade Jasper to take on another set of hurdles. Aided by his new properly fitting full-seat breeches, he was able to stay balanced in the saddle without sliding around. Surprisingly, the riding attire made a huge difference. He could move and bend in the ways he needed to when on the horse—far better than when wearing the stiff denim jeans and tennis shoes that kept causing his feet to slip out of the stirrups.

The breeches definitely helped him to stay firm in the saddle when Jasper decided to rush the first combination: two verticals positioned about four strides apart from each other. Oliver hung on as the horse misjudged the distance, put in an extra step, and lurched awkwardly over the hurdle. On the second one, they wound up taking off way too early and knocking down the rails.

Oops, that was messy.

Remembering the half halts Annamarie had taught him, Oliver gave short little tugs on the reins and slowed the horse down long enough to prepare for the next hurdle. This time he had more control, and Jasper cleared the jump without any issues. They tackled the last hurdles, and everything went beautifully as they approached them, sailed over, and landed gracefully.

Woo hoo, just finished a full course!

"Good boy!" Oliver praised Jasper and looked around to see if anybody had seen his ride, but unfortunately there was not a soul in sight. Granny had meant to come out to watch this afternoon, but she was stuck inside after being caught up in a debate with Jennifer about who knows what.

Oh well.

He patted Jasper again and let him on a loose rein to cool off. It was tempting to continue riding, but he knew better. Ending on a good note was vital, according to what his father's journal repeatedly said. Anyhow, he felt more than ready for the competition, which was next week. It was coming up fast, and he could hardly wait. The excitement was almost too much to bear. Oliver wondered whether Jennifer could relate to how he was feeling. She probably understood what it was like to be competing for the first time. Everyone had to start somewhere, including her. Maybe he'd ask her later. That is, if she wasn't still in a testy mood, which was highly probable.

Once Jasper had cooled down, Oliver cleaned him up and put him away in his stall. He quickly gave the horse a few carrots and some more pats and then headed back to the house with the anticipation of sharing what he accomplished so far. Granny would surely be proud, and maybe even Jennifer would be too. But when he sprinted to the door and opened it, he was disconcertingly greeted by the sound of Jennifer's intense squawking. Worse yet were the things she said, revealing what she and Granny had been arguing about while he had been riding.

"I can't stand him," Jennifer lamented. "I hate him!"

So it's true; she does hate me. Oliver's stomach dropped, and he was slammed with an inexplicable feeling. It was eerily familiar too, much like the sensation of hopelessness and numb grief he had felt when he'd woken up in the hospital and learned that he was the only survivor—alone, parentless, and now unwanted.

CHAPTER THIRTY-TWO

Jennifer was so fed up that she was ready to have a fit. Then again, she was *already* having a fit. Annamarie, her riding instructor who had coached her for years, had quit on her, and it was all thanks to that horrible jerk Jason. How he'd pulled it off, she wasn't sure. But it was easy to guess that since his parents owned their own riding stable, boarded horses, and even hosted competitions occasionally, Jason had been able to talk them into hiring Annamarie to train at their barn, where there was plenty of work for her due to a surplus of boarders. It would've been super easy for him; the rich snob had both his parents wrapped around his finger like thread on a spool. If he wanted something, he got it. That was actually his motto.

Not only did Jennifer feel ultimately betrayed by Annamarie, she was also panicking about the competition. How would she ever be ready in time? Pompeii was not exactly the most reliable horse, and she didn't want to look like an idiot in front of everybody again. She had been thrown off at the last show. Needless to say, it hadn't been a pleasurable experience. Jason had made fun of her about it ever since. What if Pompeii pulled another crazy stunt? She'd be the laughingstock!

Therefore, she shared her worries with her grandmother to get some peace of mind, although she was getting more worked up with each passing moment. Just the very thought of Jason made her hopping mad. Despite the endless rant, Granny listened patiently for a long time and continued to comfort her with reassuring words.

"It'll be OK. I'm sure things will work out if you give it time. You gotta hang in there and forget about him for a bit, OK?"

"But he's such a jerk. I don't know what to do anymore. It would be so much better if he didn't even live around here," Jennifer moaned, wishing Jason was somewhere else, in another state, or even a different country. On Mars if possible.

Granny was just about to reply when they both heard the back door close. It was the kind of clicking noise it made whenever somebody let it swing shut on its own. They glanced toward the kitchen and saw Oliver standing there idly, his face completely blank and void of emotion. His hands hung limply by his sides, as if he wasn't sure what to do or how to even react.

"Hey." Jennifer quickly jumped to explain. "I wasn't talking about—"

"Me? Of course you weren't," Oliver interrupted, coming to life all at once. "I'm just going to pretend I never heard that. In fact, I'll just pretend that I don't exist. Maybe that'll make it easier for you to stand me."

"Please, you don't understand!"

"What is there to understand? You've made it perfectly clear already." Shaking his head in disgust, Oliver started to stomp past, but Granny blocked him.

"I think you both should talk this out and set things right," she said firmly. "You've been tense with each other lately, and I think it's getting out of hand. In the meantime, I need to go to the other room and make a call. I'll be back shortly."

Oliver grudgingly obeyed and stayed put as Granny left, though he was still furious. To prove it, he crossed his arms and presented a venomous scowl. Trying to smooth things over, Jennifer attempted to apologize again. "Look, I really wasn't talking about you. You've completely misunderstood."

"Oh, now that you got caught talking behind my back, you're saying none of what I heard is true? That's pretty despicable."

"You've gotta believe me! I was talking about Jason. *He's* the jerk I can't stand."

"What about your annoying friend? That's not what she told me."

Good grief, he's making this so difficult, Jennifer thought to herself as she scrambled for an explanation. "Why are you bringing Lyndsey into this? Did she say something to you?"

"As a matter of fact, she did. She said I was a psyched-out throwaway that no one wanted around, and that you and Gran don't like me. Don't deny it."

"Oh no." Jennifer slapped a hand over her forehead. Lyndsey had casually mentioned that she had sorted Oliver out last night, but she never went into detail. *So that's what she meant!* Oliver was being difficult, but he never deserved to be told a bunch of lies. If anyone was an idiot, it was Lyndsey.

"I had no idea Lyndsey said those things, and I promise she just made all that stuff up. Lyndsey can be a dimwit sometimes. Surely you can agree."

But Oliver was far from convinced. With a scoff, he uncrossed his arms and asked sarcastically, "Do you want to know my opinion? I'll tell you my opinion! Honestly, I don't want to be here. I never wanted to come here."

"Um…" Jennifer struggled to respond as her cousin took the heated conversation in a totally different direction. She wasn't sure where this outburst came from. What was wrong with him? "I'm sorry that you don't like it here, but it is what it is. You need to move on."

"Move on? Ha! Maybe this'll paint the picture for you: I want everything back the way it was. I want to be back in Carolina, I want my life back, and most of all I want my family back!" Oliver spat out the words. He began to pace around the kitchen as his crabby temper boiled.

"We can't get your family back; they're gone. But you've got me and Granny. We're here for you and always will be."

"You're such a hypocrite saying *we*. Gran's been supportive, but you've done nothing but give me a hard time since I first came here."

"I never realized I was giving you a hard time. If I did, I'm really sorry." *Sheesh, why is he coming after me now? Where's Granny? Maybe she can fix this mess.*

"Of course you didn't notice! You're always so focused on yourself that you don't have a clue what it's like to lose everything you've ever known."

"Not true," Jennifer countered, all the while watching Oliver pace back and forth. It was getting rather annoying. "I know what it's like to be without parents, and it's not easy."

Oliver finally stopped near the kitchen table and glared at her angrily. "Oh, but I don't think you do," he snapped. "At least you had grandparents to live with. And didn't your mother just dump you? That's far different from having your whole family die in an instant."

OK, that's it! I'm done being nice. No one talks to me that way, Jennifer thought. "You're blowing this out of proportion. I've already said sorry and tried my best to explain things. Now you are being a jerk!"

"No, I'm not; *you* are!" Oliver retorted, raising his voice over Jennifer's. He'd balled his hands into fists as if he were ready for a fight, and he was clenching his jaw so hard that the muscles in his cheeks were bulging. Jennifer had never seen him this agitated before. Somehow it seemed that he had been in a dormant state, biding his time until he had an excuse to explode. Apparently this argument was the perfect trigger.

Jennifer wasn't one to back off though. She lifted her chin and squared her shoulders stubbornly. "You're always locked away in that delusional mind of yours, moaning and whining about what you no longer have. Why don't you just get over it? Can't you make a new life for yourself?"

Upon hearing this, something in Oliver's face snapped, and for a brief second, he didn't say anything. The silence that swelled between them was very unsettling. Now Jennifer knew she had crossed the line.

Suddenly, he drew a deep breath and yelled at the top of his lungs so loudly that the walls shook, and the scream echoed throughout the house. Jennifer could almost see the back of his throat. Then just as abruptly, he grabbed a wooden kitchen chair and hurled it clear across the room. It struck a window of all things, creating a horrendous racket. Shattered glass exploded in all directions, raining down onto the tile floor like crystallized snowflakes.

"You see that?" Oliver shouted, pointing to the broken window and chair. *"That's* what has become of me! I'm fractured beyond repair and useless."

What's got into him? Has he gone mad?

Jennifer was too stunned to even speak. She didn't bother trying either. Obviously anything she said would make the situation worse. But whether she spoke or not, Oliver's temper tantrum wasn't over yet. Before she could stop him, he reached for a different chair and held it high above his head. Letting out another manic yell, he threw it hard. The chair whizzed past Jennifer, close enough that she felt a gust of wind. It hit the wall and left behind an ugly dent.

Oh my God, I'm going to get killed! "Cut it out!" she demanded. "You've made your point."

"No, I haven't! Nobody gets it, certainly not *you!*"

"What in the world is going on in here?" Granny came into the kitchen, looking around in bewilderment. She gasped and quickly dodged a third chair that Oliver had tossed in her direction without realizing she was there. It was the fastest Jennifer had ever seen her move. "Oliver, stop this instant! You're going to hurt someone!"

But Oliver didn't seem to register Granny's chiding and continued to rage, stomping all the way to the other side of the kitchen table. "'Get over it,' everyone says. 'Face it,' everyone says. If anyone's delusional, it's them! *They* are the idiots!"

Granny inched toward him cautiously and said in the most soothing way possible, "Look, you need to calm down—"

"No! I'm tired of not being listened to," Oliver yelled, taking hold of the side of the table and flipping it over. One of its legs broke off from the impact. "I'm tired of being ignored. Nothing I say ever matters!"

"There are better ways to deal with this. We can all sit down quietly in the living room and discuss anything you'd like."

"Yeah," Jennifer chimed in. "Look at yourself. You're going berserk!"

"I know how that'll go. You'll just tell me to face reality and accept it. Well, I already know what it is, and it's heartbreaking. I hate reality!"

To Jennifer's surprise, Oliver's voice started to crack unexpectedly, and his eyes grew watery. Was he about to cry? In a tone that was barely audible, he murmured, "I can't take it anymore," and he darted out the back door in a flash.

Then just like that, the meltdown was over. A quietness hung in the air as if nothing had happened. But unfortunately the damage was done. The table was on its side, chairs were lying where they had been flung about, and broken glass glittered against the tile under the window that now needed to be replaced. Plus, there were two caved-in spots where a couple of the chairs had hit the wall.

"What a mess. I guess the argument was kind of my fault." Jennifer felt bad for all the trouble she had caused. Worst yet, she hadn't been fair to her cousin. He was right—she didn't understand how he felt at all.

"Yes, it is to an extent—but not completely," Granny stated as she found a broom and started sweeping up the glass. "Oliver was already upset to begin with."

"What do you mean?"

"He didn't want to let go and move on. I heard you from the other room, telling him he had to do just that."

I suppose she's right, Jennifer realized. *If he needs me to be there for him, now's the time.* Without wasting another second to explain what she was doing, she headed out the door to find him.

CHAPTER THIRTY-THREE

The thick, stuffy smell in the barn was the only thing that kept Oliver aware of where he was headed. Everything else was a complete blur of distorted shapes and colors. Nothing made sense anymore. He felt as if he had been gutted and all his problems were laid out in the open for everyone to see. His emotions were especially a mess, jumbled up and scythed into unravelling threads that he couldn't quite reel back in.

But at this point, it felt easier to let them stay that way, shredded and exposed. Why keep fighting? It didn't really matter. Oliver was mentally and physically exhausted. The ongoing battle of trying not to fall apart was wearing him down. Ever since the accident, he had kept everything pent up inside until he simply couldn't hold it in any longer. When Jennifer told him the blunt truth and opened the floodgates, he completely lost control. He just flipped, feeling an extreme urgency to get all frustrations out.

Wanting nothing more than to be with his only friend, Oliver found Jasper's stall and slipped in. The horse looked on curiously as he stumbled through and collapsed at the back of the stall, sinking into the cushy shavings that seemed to receive him sympathetically. With a sigh, he leaned back against the wall. The wooden panels felt rough and scratchy, but at least they were softer than what words could be.

Jasper seemed to notice that something was amiss and ambled over to where Oliver was sitting. Then he dropped his head and snorted inquisitively, as if to say, "What are you doing down there?"

"I feel so alone right now," Oliver whispered, reaching up to pet the horse's nose. The warm breaths that blew out of his nostrils were comforting against Oliver's face. "I really miss my family..." He trailed off, unable to say another word. It hurt too much.

Oliver couldn't stop the sudden onset of despair that consumed him. His throat burned as if he had swallowed molten lava, and the sensation oozed rapidly into his chest. The continuous ringing in his ears intensified so much that it was the only thing he could hear. He wondered whether or not he could recover. It was doubtful. The pain that had dulled was now a bleeding wound again and rawer than ever.

Overwhelmed, he brought both knees up to his chest so that they shielded his wrenching heart. After having held himself together for so long, refusing to feel the grief, he finally cracked. His eyes welled up against his will, and every broken piece of him started to fall in the form of tears. As the sobs choked him, he buried his face, wishing he could dissolve into the ground and escape the misery. If this was what everything was going to come down to, he wasn't sure he had the will to fight anymore. The agony was unbearable.

Then out of nowhere, a pair of arms wrapped around Oliver and embraced him in a tight hug. Not caring who it was, he leaned into the person, seeking the warmth and love he had missed so desperately.

"I'm here." Jennifer's voice reassured him. "It's gonna be OK."

Those simple words were what he had needed to hear ever since the accident—just to be told that he would be OK, to be given a reason to hope. Though one question always bothered him. Anxious to get it off his chest, he asked, "Why did I have to be the only one to survive?"

"You were just lucky I guess."

"Sometimes I wish I hadn't been," Oliver admitted, wiping his eyes with the back of his hand. The tears still rolled consistently down his cheeks. "My sister's gone;

my mom and dad are gone. How can I ever enjoy life without them? It isn't fair."

"It's not fair at all. But stuff happens, and you've just gotta find a way to work through it."

"I don't know if I can."

"Hey, look at me."

Oliver lifted his head and met Jennifer's intent gaze, her vibrant green eyes and wild red hair that accentuated her freckles glowed in the shaft of light that reached through the stall window. "Yeah?"

"I can't replace your sister or your parents, but I can definitely be your cousin. I'll be there to help you every step of the way. You're like a brother to me, and I love you just as much as one too. I want you to always remember that, OK?"

"I don't know what I'd do without you." It was all Oliver could think of to say as he hugged her back. In that moment, he felt steadier somehow and less like the dregs of the past, cast aside to dissipate.

━◄┼ ┼►━

Later, after things had settled down, Oliver helped to clean up the mess in the kitchen. It was the least he could do after having had that embarrassing outburst, which he deeply regretted. Granny didn't appear to be overly concerned though. She simply supplied him with a few tools and then instructed him in how to reattach the leg to the table and repair the dents in the wall.

Oliver didn't have a lot of experience with tools, and his craftsmanship wasn't exactly great, but he gladly tried anyway. He was in the middle of smearing remarkably sticky putty over a dent when Granny came into the kitchen to check up on him. A glimmer of amusement in her eyes showed as she analyzed the work. "I see you've filled in the holes."

The repair job was a disaster, really; the off-white gooey paste was messy beyond belief, making it impossible to keep it from splattering everywhere. It had dribbled all over the floor and streaked across the wall, so the fist-size dent wound up looking like pigeons had pooped there for the last decade.

"Uh, yeah." Oliver wiped his hands on his shirt in an effort get the gunk off. His clothes were already caked with putty anyway, so staining them was no longer a concern. "I think I'm making a bigger mess though."

"Don't worry about it. Next time Stanley comes to visit, I'll have him take a look. I'm sure he will be happy to show you how to finish patching the holes."

Awesome, she's letting me off the hook. It had been a pretty long day, and Oliver couldn't wait to put his feet up and relax a little. But he wasn't quite ready to make an escape yet. There were still unanswered questions, and since it was just the two of them together, it felt like a good time to ask. Jennifer had stayed behind in the barn and was preparing to ride her horse this afternoon. All in all, it was a perfect opportunity.

"Um, Gran? I was wondering about something…"

"Yes?"

"You never explained about my dad. I mean why did he stop riding and never come here to visit?"

Granny tilted her head back slightly as if she were caught off guard by the question. Then with a pensive nod, she gestured to the living room, saying, "Come with me, and I'll explain."

They moved into the other room, and Granny waited until they were both seated before she spoke again. "I don't know if you realize this, but your daddy was one of the top riders in the nation."

"Really? I read his journal and imagined he must have been pretty good—but top in the nation? That's pretty cool."

"When your daddy and your uncle Stanley were still little boys, your granddad let them ride some of his retired competition horses here at the farm. As they got the hang of it, he got them some younger jumping horses and started coaching them to enter the local shows. From there, their riding just took off like a wildfire."

"What about Jennifer's mom; did she ride too?"

"Alice was younger than the boys, but when she did get old enough to try riding, she didn't take a liking to it. Alice and the boys were so different from one another. All the boys wanted to do was be outside with the horses, while she was always much happier indoors, spending her time reading a book."

"I guess she didn't really have anything in common with the family, did she?"

"No, she was out on a different path, with big dreams of going to college and making a career for herself," Granny said somewhat vaguely, as if she didn't want to go into detail.

"Oh, OK." Realizing Granny didn't want to keep talking about Jennifer's mother, Oliver changed the subject. "So who was a better rider, my dad or Uncle Stanley?"

"The boys were both good, but when it came to competing, Daniel had that little bit of something extra. It sure was something to watch him ride. He swept up every competition in the show-jumping circuit. Of course, the more he won, the more his name was known. Our boarding business started to boom, and your granddad had many riding students. Stanley even began to help out a little, and he discovered he had knack for teaching more so than competing."

"Why aren't all the riders here now?" Oliver asked. "Why don't you still board?"

"I'm getting to that part. Everything was going along wonderfully. We had a thriving business, and both sons were happy; your grandfather couldn't have asked for more. No one expected it, but the economy around here took a big downturn, and jobs started drying up.

Boarders couldn't afford to keep their horses or take lessons."

"So, what happened?"

"Well, it was like watching a house of cards begin to collapse. One thing led to another. Our debt started to pile up. We tried cutting back on costs, which meant that we had to cut corners on staff and maintenance. What few boarders we had left just didn't pay enough to cover the expense of running a thirty-five-stall barn and a covered arena—"

"What? There's only eight stalls out there! And I certainly don't see a covered arena." *Is she loony or something?* Oliver wondered.

Reading his mind, Granny chuckled. "Calm down; I haven't gone senile yet. I told you we had a thriving business. Back then we had expanded and built a big barn with a covered arena alongside it. That barn you see out there now was our personal barn. Anyway, our show-jumping stable sure was an impressive setup. Hard come, easy go though."

Her craggy face, which was lined with years of worry and exhaustion, looked pained, as if she were reliving the tragedy again. She exhaled before relinquishing the rest of the untold history.

"It didn't take but a split second for that fire to rip through the barn and into the arena. We barely had enough time to save the horses. The insurance people found out that the fire started because we had not fixed the breaker box when it needed new wiring. So they didn't cover the claims. We were left with no money to rebuild any of it. All we had was a big pile of charred wood and ashes."

Oliver stayed quiet, sensing that this was not the time to ask more questions. Instead he sat still on the couch and listened intently as Granny continued talking.

"You know, thinking back on the fire all these years later, I figure it was the true turning point that led to the break in our family. There was one hope left. The USEF National Show-Jumping Championships was a few months away, and the winnings would've been enough to scrape things back together. We used the last of our savings just to get to the event. Suddenly, the future of our barn and our livelihood was pinned on your daddy's shoulders. We all hoped Daniel would win, bring home the award money, and save our family from bankruptcy."

"Did he win?" Oliver asked, no longer able to contain himself. By now he was sitting on the edge of the couch, eager to know how the story would unfold. "Surely he did..."

Granny shook her head sadly. "Everyone's moods changed. Fueled by desperation, your granddad coached Daniel relentlessly in the short time before the competition. When they weren't training in the arena, Daniel exercised rigorously so he would be in shape. Everything was intense. They were consumed with getting ready for the competition. Your granddad wanted everything to be perfect for the big day. I still don't know how he got the money, but he surprised Daniel with the most beautiful show coat I had ever seen. When your father put that coat on and got on his horse, he had the world by the tail.

"Sometimes, though, no matter how prepared a person is physically, they still have to be able to handle the pressure mentally, and that was where your father was not ready. He couldn't deal with knowing all that was at stake, and he let fear set in as he rode into that arena. He made his first lap around and lined up for the first jump. Everything depended on him pulling off a clear run. I could almost see the fear eating into his thoughts. Of course, Daniel's horse picked up on his nerves and faltered, knocking down the poles.

"From there on, Daniel made mistake after mistake. Each fault whittled down his confidence until he was so nervous and distracted that he wound up being disqualified for too many refusals. The one competition he absolutely *had* to win went down the drain. In the end we were forced to sell all the horses, including Daniel's. He swore off riding afterward because he felt responsible for losing the only chance the family had left.

"Watching everything fall apart angered your granddad and caused big fights between him and Daniel. They each blamed the other, thinking the loss of the competition could have been prevented somehow.

Stanley was caught in the middle, being used as a scapegoat for their anger. The two of them never could settle their disagreements, so eventually Daniel moved away. Sometimes he came back to visit me and Stanley, but only when your granddad was out of town. As the years passed, though, your dad stopped coming. I'm not really sure why. I suppose seeing what he'd left behind bothered him too much."

"But he never wanted to ride again? He just quit?" Oliver asked. "I don't understand why he'd stop because of one competition."

"It wasn't just about one competition. Your father couldn't deal with the guilt he felt over all that happened," Granny said, summing up the story. "I reckon leaving was his way of punishing himself."

No wonder he didn't tell me he used to compete, Oliver thought to himself as he mulled over the story of his father. It had a disappointing ending, but it was sort of a relief to finally know everything. Plus, it was a strong reminder for him to put aside distress and push forward during challenging times. Above all, keeping a tight bond with one's family for support always helped whenever there was a bump in the road.

CHAPTER THIRTY-FOUR

A fter such a chaotic day, and still a bit rattled by her cousin's epic meltdown, Jennifer kept quiet, feeling as though she were walking on eggshells. The last thing she wanted to do was start another fight. Oliver had the same impression and gave her a wide berth as well. Not surprisingly, he had no trouble concealing himself and disappearing without so much as a trace. Living with him was like living with a ghost at times. Today, however, he may as well have been an enraged banshee. He had raised such a ruckus that the neighbors—who were half a mile away—had probably overheard it.

It wasn't until dinner that Jennifer finally saw him again. For a few awkward moments, she, Granny, and

Oliver sat at the kitchen table and ate in silence, lost in their own thoughts. Tonight's meal was fried chicken, with mashed potatoes and brussels sprouts on the side. She didn't care much for the vegetables. It seemed like Granny tried to smuggle them into their food every chance she got. They always tasted disgustingly bland, except for onions. Those typically had a nasty, somewhat-bitter aftertaste.

Jennifer stifled a chuckle when she glanced over and saw Oliver slowly picking through the round pale-green balls on his plate. He tried to spear one with his fork, but it bounced off and fell into his lap. Pretending not to notice, he stabbed at another one. This time it stuck. With no other choice, he reluctantly put the brussels sprout in his mouth. His face scrunched up like wadded paper. Thinking that nobody was watching, he grabbed a napkin and discreetly spat it out.

Why didn't I think of that trick? Jennifer wondered. Apparently she wasn't the only one with a grudge against vegetables. Since Oliver was sitting just across from her, she reached out with her foot and nudged him under the table. Puzzled, he looked up.

"Watch this," Jennifer mouthed, taking her fork and collecting a brussels sprout. She stuffed it into the mashed potatoes to disguise the flavor. It was her favorite method of consuming vegetables without having to suffer as much.

Oliver got the message and smiled gratefully. "Thanks," he mouthed back. Now they were both teaming up against Granny. She definitely had her work cut out for her, and she didn't even know it. How cunningly perfect. Better yet, things were all right between Jennifer and Oliver, without question or doubt. Knowing that they were on good terms again was a relief.

Suddenly realizing something was going on, Granny stopped eating and spoke up from her seat at the head of the table. "What are you two smiling about?"

With an expression on his face that exclaimed, *busted!* Oliver returned to eating his food. He acted as if he were unaware of anyone else while he painstakingly picked through the vegetables again.

"N...nothing. We're simply enjoying our meal," Jennifer fibbed. Thinking quickly, she decided to broach the subject about the situation of not having a trainer. It was a good distraction. Besides, it was important to sort the issue out sooner rather than later. "Say, what are we going to do about the fact that we don't have a trainer? The competition is coming up fast, and there's no way we can find another one before then."

"Hmm, good point." Granny contemplated for a brief second with a smile. "Though there's no need to worry. That call I made earlier was to Uncle Stanley. He has agreed to help out with training you guys. How does that sound?"

"Wait, he knows how to teach?"

"Of course he does! He learned just as much as Daniel did about horses from your grandfather. They were brothers. Don't you kids ever put two and two together?

"I never really thought about it I guess. But sure, that sounds like a great idea. We can give him a shot." Jennifer grinned at the thought of having her uncle help her and Oliver prepare for the competition. Everything appeared to fall into place now that they had a solution.

Apparently it had taken some considerable effort to convince Uncle Stanley to come out and teach because, like his brother, he had abandoned riding. But he eventually agreed to help Jennifer and Oliver on the condition that it would be a one-time thing since there was not much time to prepare for the upcoming competition. After that, they would be on their own until they found a new trainer.

Beggars can't be choosers, Jennifer thought. At least Uncle Stanley would be her and Oliver's trainer for the time being, even if it was only until the competition.

Granny was right about Uncle Stanley. He really did know quite a lot about riding; he instructed just as well as Annamarie, if not better. Uncle Stanley's instructions were clear, concise, and straight to the point, unlike Annamarie, who tended to chatter during lessons. The best part was that he came over every single afternoon instead of just on the weekends. It was especially interesting to see Uncle Stanley teach Oliver through-out the week, but even more so to learn new techniques, which helped immensely.

Maybe that spoiled snob Jason had done everyone a favor without even realizing it. Jennifer smiled every time she thought about this delicious fact.

Ha, last laugh's on him!

CHAPTER THIRTY-FIVE

"What's takin' so long, *city boy?*" Jennifer's drawling accent penetrated Oliver's clouded mind and brought him back to earth. "You've been at it for almost an hour now. Are you done yet?" She chided impatiently as she buzzed around his room, picking up the clothes he had left strewn on the floor.

"Done with what?" Oliver stared at her absentmindedly. He was having a hard time wrapping his mind around the fact that it was time to leave for the competition—well, almost. Everyone would be departing the house early next morning. The days had flown by so fast it was unbelievable. However, his nerves didn't go away as quickly. Anxiety flopped about in his stomach, writhing and clawing its way up his throat. It steadily got worse while he stood by his bed where his suitcase lay, still depressingly empty.

"I'm going to puke," he said, fretting.

Jennifer rolled her eyes and dumped Oliver's clothes on the bed. "You're supposed to be packing. But making a mess is all you've accomplished so far."

"I'm not sure what to take." *Man, I feel sick.* Oliver wasn't sure how much longer he could keep everything down. He clutched his stomach and tried to not think about it.

"Oh, good grief. It's not rocket science. All you need is your toothbrush and enough clothes to last for four days, including riding pants and a show coat. And maybe something to entertain yourself with during the trip, like your iPod, or maybe even a good old-fashioned book."

"I don't feel ready. What if I mess up?"

Jennifer laughed aloud at his comment. "You can't mess up packing. Just take what you wanna bring."

"I meant the competition." Oliver swallowed back the bile that started to bubble up. It tasted horrifically bitter. Now he really had an urge to gag. "I'm kind of nervous," he admitted.

"Don't be. You'll do just fine. Having fun is what matters here."

"What if I freak out…like my dad did?"

"And what if you fall off?" Jennifer promptly answered him with a question. "What if you go out there, crash through every fence, and make a fool of yourself? Or maybe you'll get laughed at."

"That would be pretty lousy."

"Well, there are a lot of what ifs. You can't predict what's going to happen tomorrow—or the day after. Whatever happens, it'll be OK. It's just up to you to sit back and enjoy the ride. Quit stressing yourself out so much."

"I can't help it. I don't want to flub everything up."

"So what? Who cares if you flub up or not? Relax!" Grinning mischievously, Jennifer added, "If you gotta puke, go ahead. You're looking pretty green."

Oliver moaned inwardly with exasperation. Why was she always so frank? Somehow she kept coming up with the best remarks, either insulting enough to tear through flesh or inspirational enough to move mountains.

"Hey, I'll help you pack." Jennifer picked some shirts off the bed and held them up for Oliver to see. "Which one do you wanna bring along?"

Oliver grinned. The tension in his stomach eased a little. His cousin was eccentric, but she was the best friend he could ever ask for. She was right; what did it matter whether he won or not at the competition? *So what?* He had already trained with Uncle Stanley and was more than ready. There was nothing to worry about. Now was the time to have fun.

"I'll take that one," he said, pointing to one of the shirts.

Together they worked, packing everything and getting ready for the early morning that would come. Time, the only predictable thing in Oliver's life nowadays, moved quite quickly, and it was soon bedtime. He was sure everything was set to go for the morning, but something important seemed to be missing. But what? This bothered him to no end. Fortunately, Granny already had it covered. Just as Oliver was about to call it a day and turn out the lights, she knocked on his bedroom door.

"Are you ready for tomorrow?" she asked when he let her in.

Oliver nodded drowsily in response and then went and flopped onto his bed. Sleep was the only thing he could think about right now, precious, precious sleep. Why on earth was Granny keeping him up? Wasn't she as tired as he was?

Ugh, so exhausted.

Granny chuckled at his melodrama and informed him that she would only be a moment. "Actually, I want to give you something," she said, revealing a bundled object and handing it over. Surprised, Oliver quickly sat up and accepted the gift. It had a square shape, and it was carefully wrapped in aged light-brown paper that was crinkly to the touch. A piece of frayed twine had been wound around the fragile package, keeping it sealed. Whatever was inside, it was quite treasured.

"What is it?" Oliver questioned, unsure of what he might discover.

Granny pursed her lips, refusing to tell him. "Open it and find out," she insisted.

Oliver cautiously untied the twine and peeled away the paper. At first glance, he was surprised to find what looked like a sports jacket tucked neatly inside the package. As he finished unwrapping the gift, it dawned on him what he was actually holding—a show coat. Not just any show coat, though, but a very unique and expensive one.

The fabric was as pitch black as a clear night sky. Polished silver buttons glistened like stars down the front of the jacket and along the cuffs. The collar and the pocket flaps were a deep scarlet red, the same color as the silky lining inside the coat, and decked with white piping.

Too stunned to even think, Oliver held the coat gingerly in his hands to avoid wrinkling it. He had never seen any item of clothing so intricately detailed. He gazed at the coat for a long time. When he was finally able to take his eyes off it, he looked up at Granny. "This was my dad's coat, wasn't it?"

"Indeed it was." Granny spoke quietly, as if she were in a church. For a brief second, she appeared to be saddened by the statement, but then a warm smile crept up and washed away the hint of sorrow. "It's yours now though."

Oliver hesitated, shocked that Granny would even consider giving him such a valued heirloom. "W...wow, are you sure? I don't deserve this..."

Nodding reassuringly, Granny patted him on the shoulder. "Your father would have wanted you to have it."

"Thanks, Gran. I don't know what to say. This is amazing."

CHAPTER THIRTY-SIX

The morning arrived quickly. It was so early that the sky was still dark from the sun's absence, but the house was already coming alive as everyone began to stir. There were a lot of things that needed to be done in a very short amount of time; it was a going to be a six-hour drive, since the competition was out of town.

For Jennifer and Granny, waking up at odd hours was an old routine. The horse shows tended to be several hours away. That was one of the perks of living out in the country. If they left early, they would arrive at the competition grounds by midafternoon, which would provide enough time to settle the horses into their assigned stalls and get checked in for the competition.

The plan was that Uncle Stanley would come over with his truck to help hook up the trailer and load the horses, which would give everyone a head start. In the meantime, Jennifer and Granny focused on prepping the horses while Oliver started working on his list of things to do. But it turned out that early mornings, city boys deprived of sleep, and complicated lists didn't quite mix well. Jennifer soon got sucked into having to multitask by supervising her cousin as she worked. It wasn't the easiest thing to do, especially when it involved having to explain things over and over.

"To measure out the food, you have to count the days that we'll be away from home," Jennifer said for what felt like the thousandth time as she tried her best to show Oliver how to sort the food. It was pretty simple. All he had to do was measure the grain and dump it into individual resealable plastic bags. Irritatingly enough, he just wasn't getting it for some reason.

"See, you have to remember that the horses get fed in the morning, at noon, and at dinnertime." Jennifer picked up a plastic bag and held it in front of Oliver's lethargic face. He blinked his bloodshot eyes a couple of times to register what she was saying.

"All right, they get fed three times a day. What time is it, by the way?"

"It's five o'clock, and we've gotta leave in about an hour." Sighing, Jennifer continued, "Each bag is already labeled with the time and the horse's name. It's very simple. Pompeii gets two scoops in morning…"

She paused when she realized her cousin was obviously not comprehending what she was saying because he just stared blankly. Testing to see whether he was even listening or not, Jennifer casually said, "The horses will also need some silverware to eat their food. Do you think you could grab a set of forks, spoons, and knives from the kitchen before we leave?"

"OK," Oliver said compliantly, without giving her words a second thought. Then he yawned loudly. His mucky morning breath made Jennifer wince. "How many scoops per horse, again?"

Good grief. This is just not working.

Jennifer concluded that her cousin was a hopeless case and gave up. Besides, if he was that tired, it would be safer to handle the feed herself. Otherwise, the horses could get colic or something. "Actually, I'll take care of it. Why don't you go and set some bales of hay and alfalfa by the trailer? When Uncle Stanley arrives, you can chuck them into the back of his truck."

"Uncle Stanley's coming?" Oliver asked, failing to remember what had been planned out for the departure.

"Ugh, just get the hay and alfalfa!" Exasperated, Jennifer waved her hands and shooed Oliver off. "Go! We don't have much time left. And find Creature for me, will you?"

As soon as Uncle Stanley came rolling up the driveway in his battered Chevrolet, things went into full gear, and everyone started to hustle. Granny assisted Uncle Stanley with the trailer, getting it hooked up and ready to go. At the same time, Jennifer busied herself with putting the shipping boots on the horses, all the while trying to keep an eye on her sleepy cousin, who still continued to trudge around like a listless zombie. To say the least, he wasn't of much use this morning. Although he did find Creature in the end. The energetic dog bounced around, struggling to break free of the leash that held him captive. But Oliver seemed totally unaware of the commotion and just kept a tight grip.

Finally it was time to load the horses. By then Oliver was somewhat alert enough to manage Jasper. Having gone to countless shows before, Jasper calmly stepped into the trailer and waited patiently as Oliver fiddled with the lead rope and tied it correctly after a few failed attempts.

Pompeii was a whole other story. The madcap horse balked at the first sight of the trailer. Digging his heels into the dirt, he refused to take another step closer. Jennifer pulled hard on the lead. Pompeii began to back up, dragging her with him. She tugged on the lead and quickly turned the horse around, making a large arc so they would be facing the trailer again. This time Pompeii took a few hesitant steps forward and then did a fake out by skidding to the side and plunging past the trailer rather than going up the ramp. Eventually, Jennifer did get her stubborn horse onto the trailer, but only after Uncle Stanley approached from behind and gave Pompeii some convincing taps on the rump with a lunge whip.

Once everything was set to go, everyone piled into Uncle Stanley's Chevrolet. The prehistoric truck groaned and moaned when he turned over the engine. Agonizing under the weight of the trailer carrying two horses, it slowly crept out of the driveway and then puttered down the tree-lined road. Taking a quick peek out the window from the back seat, Jennifer saw the first glimpse of dawn breaking through the dark. Orange rays of light fingered their way past the thick branches of the trees and shined into the truck's cab. Jennifer then looked over at her cousin, who was sitting next to her. The light hit his hair perfectly, illuminating it so that it took on a golden sheen. It almost looked like a lion's mane, the way it bushed out and then sort of curled at the ends, halfway down the back of his neck.

"How are you doing?" Jennifer asked. Judging from her past experiences of riding in the car with Oliver, she wondered how he would fare on a long road trip.

"I'm fine, just very sleepy right now." Oliver gave a partial grin and slumped drowsily in his seat. He showed no signs of being anxious about being in the pickup truck, which put Jennifer's concern to rest. "I'm pretty excited about the competition. I wonder what it'll be like."

"Oh, it's going to be amazing. You'll love it; just you wait and see." Jennifer smiled and thought back to all the times she had competed. "There's nothing like the sensation of soaring over those jumps and crossing the finish line. Then the crowd cheers and claps, your friends shout out your name, and the whole world stops for a few seconds."

"Sounds incredible."

"It really is. I think you're going to have the time of your life." Jennifer sighed happily and mulled over the feeling of anticipation that was already building up inside of her. What would the competition be like this time? Each one was always different, whether it was exciting, very stressful, packed with fun, or challenging. But one thing all the competitions had in common was that they were all memorable.

Noticing that Oliver had suddenly gone quiet, Jennifer glanced in his direction. She couldn't help but chuckle. Her cousin was slumped against the pickup's door and dead asleep. The faint sound of his snoring slowly filled the inside of the cab, enveloping everyone in a somewhat peaceful aura.

CHAPTER THIRTY-SEVEN

During the majority of the trip, Uncle Stanley talked about the competition. He explained in depth what everyone's roles would be and what to expect when they got there. Oliver had no idea that quiet Uncle Stanley could be so talkative. It was as if he had been keeping to himself and the excitement of going to the competition had suddenly compelled him to chatter incessantly. According to Jennifer, when Oliver asked discreetly, Uncle Stanley always did this every time he helped trailer her horse to a competition.

Although it was interesting to listen to Uncle Stanley, it got a little tiring after a while. Eventually Oliver tuned out his voice as the countryside drew his attention.

Thousands of cattle dotted their pastures, which were surrounded by miles of fences. Occasionally, he would spot small herds of horses grazing in separate pastures. In the distance, there would sometimes be an old, dilapidated barn to shelter them whenever rain or snow happened to fall. There was something different about these horses; they were rugged, weathered horses that lived without the luxuries Oliver's and Jennifer's horses had. They didn't get groomed, petted, loved, or ridden daily. Though their lives were entirely different, they weren't necessarily bad. These horses got to roam freely throughout seemingly endless acres of tall grass, doing whatever they pleased. It was kind of interesting to think about.

Oliver was quite startled when he was suddenly jarred awake. He hadn't realized he had dozed off again. Groaning, he forced his eyes open. The first thing he saw was Jennifer's eager face, brightened with an ear-to-ear smile.

"Wake up!" she said excitedly. "We're here!" Trying to ensure that Oliver didn't fall back asleep, she grabbed his shoulder and shook him vigorously. There was no ignoring her.

"OK, OK, I'm awake!" Oliver sputtered, waving his arms in an effort to fend her off. Granny, who was sitting up front, turned in her seat and enthusiastically stated that it was time to get the horses unloaded.

"Yeah," Jennifer chimed in. "Uncle Stanley's already gone to sign in. We need to get moving."

To add to all the commotion, Creature decided that he couldn't stand being in the truck any longer. He began to bark and jump around, scratching Oliver and Jennifer with his claws in the process. Dog hair flew everywhere and created a reddish cloud above their heads. In turn, Jennifer started fussing at Creature, commanding him to behave. Of course, the lunatic dog did not listen. His barking got more intense and drowned out Jennifer's voice, as well as Granny's when she pitched in with a few stern words of her own.

Oh jeez, I should've stayed asleep

Wanting no part of the chaos, Oliver bailed out of the truck and left the quarreling trio to their own fates. He was quite surprised when he saw that it was even more hectic outside. Nothing could have prepared him for the electric atmosphere of a horse show teeming with activity.

The show ground was abuzz; dogs weaved in and out of the crowds, tagging along behind noisy children. Anxious horses jigged, tossing their heads as their handlers unloaded them out of trailers and led them across the parking lot. Neighs rang out frantically as each horse announced its presence. Everyone hurried back and forth from the barn that the horses would be staying in overnight. The barn was huge, dwarfing the massive oak trees that were sprawled around it. Bordered by planted flowers, a detailed cobblestone path led the way through the mahogany doors that had been pushed open invitingly. There was no doubt that barn was just as elegant inside.

Oliver stared with awe at the whole scene, marveling over the magnificent layout. "This is amazing," he said aloud, not expecting Uncle Stanley to come up from behind to give him a walloping pat on the back. It was strong enough to almost knock the breath out of Oliver. A tingle ricocheted from the uncannily familiar touch and made his skin itch. The only other person who used to whap him affectionately on the back like that had been his father.

"It is, isn't it?" Uncle Stanley said, responding to Oliver's statement. Deep in thought, he took his calloused hand and rubbed it over his gray mustache. It had become somewhat thicker since the first time they had met. It seemed like ages ago.

"Yeah, it's incredible…" *Incredible how much can change and still be the same in its own way.*

Already sensing the excitement of the horse show, Pompeii shifted his weight around and rocked the trailer. Mellow Jasper suddenly decided he wasn't going to tolerate his annoying travel companion anymore, and he kicked the sides a couple of times to let everyone know. Uncle Stanley snapped out of his trance and jumped into action. "Let's get those horses unloaded. They're about to jump out of their skins."

While Uncle Stanley went to help Granny unload the pickup truck, Jennifer and Oliver quickly got the horses out of the trailer. As usual, Jasper behaved like a saint, whereas Pompeii hurtled backward down the ramp. Barely controlled by the lead that Jennifer held on to, he opened his mouth and bellowed like a stallion. He then spun around and dragged a flailing Jennifer halfway down the parking lot, intending to attack the luxurious carpet of green grass by the barn.

Jennifer had to use all of her strength to rein back the gray monster and steer him in the right direction. Despite her efforts, the horse managed to snatch one of the potted flowers residing in the doorway, ripping it up by the roots. He raised his head and held his prize out of reach when Jennifer tried to grab it.

Keeping a safe distance from the sideshow, Oliver followed behind with Jasper in tow. As expected, the inside of the barn was a work of art. Chandeliers hung from the ceiling, lighting up the wide aisle. The floor was made out of russet-colored rubber bricks, custom made so the horses wouldn't slip. The wooden stall doors were polished, along with their brass hardware and the shiny black cast-iron bars on each stall divider, which provided decent ventilation for the breeze to flow through easily.

By the time the horses were settled into their assigned stalls, Uncle Stanley and Granny came trundling down the barn aisle with two large trunks that had all the tack, grooming supplies, and other necessities. Flopping about on the end of his leash was none other than Creature, still trying to find a way to escape his current captor, Uncle Stanley. At one point, Creature planted his feet and absolutely refused to move, but Uncle Stanley hardly took notice and kept on walking, dragging the poor dog along.

"This is just about everything," Uncle Stanley announced, handing Creature over to Jennifer. "There are still a few things left in the truck, though, so your grandmother and I will be right back."

As soon as Granny and Uncle Stanley left, Jennifer picked up a couple of plastic buckets and said she was going to fill them with water. Walking past Oliver, she threw the end of Creature's leash in his direction, automatically assigning him to dog-walking duty. The dog glanced around wildly when he realized his person had abandoned him. Then he lunged forward, croaking out strangled barks as he attempted to choke himself by pulling on his collar.

Ugh, stupid dog. Oliver wrapped the leash around his hand to keep from losing his grip. His fingers started to turn red as the circulation was soon cut off. "How long will it be until we get to the hotel?" he asked when Jennifer got back.

Jennifer sighed at his impatience. "We'll be done in an hour or so. Go ahead and tie Creature and help me get all this stuff set up."

Eager to do something other than stand around with the dog, Oliver tied Creature's leash to one of the tack trunks and got to work. First he helped to hang the buckets of water in the stalls, along with two extra buckets for food later. After that he and Jennifer started to sort out the bedding. Both horses got three bags of wood shavings for their stalls. Oliver opened the bags, dumped the shavings, and spread them out with a pitchfork. Meanwhile, Jennifer organized the tack and grooming supplies and also checked the schedules for the classes. Uncle Stanley and Granny managed to return with the rest of the stuff, and then they left again to park the trailer.

During all of these activities, Creature whined incessantly because he was being ignored. He grew more agitated by the minute, whimpering louder and louder until he was barking. Despite getting hushed several times, he wouldn't be quiet. Jennifer soon got sick of the noise and ordered Oliver to do something useful and go walk the dog. Like always, she ignored the glare that he answered her with.

Grumbling under his breath, Oliver obeyed. He tugged on Creature's leash and ambled down the barn aisle. Rather than walk in a straight line, Creature zigzagged all over the place, investigating every inch of the ground. There were multiple instances when he made laps around Oliver's legs, entangling them with the leash each time; then they would have to stop to get untangled.

They made it outside the barn finally, and Oliver directed Creature to a large grassy area a few feet away. Creature realized where they were heading and made a beeline for it, yanking and tugging on the leash. Oliver had to use all of his weight to hold the fervent dog back. For a dog with stubby legs and large clumsy paws, he was pretty strong. Then again, he and Pompeii were Jennifer's two precious heathens, demented to the cores of their broken brains. Jennifer had mentioned wanting a barn cat in the near future. Oliver dreaded seeing what something with claws and an inherent desire to murder small animals for sport would be capable of.

"Hurry up already," Oliver muttered as he waited for Creature to pick a spot to do his business. Of course the dog took his time to scrutinize each miserable blade of grass. After about ten minutes of sniffing around, he sneezed indignantly and looked up at Oliver with his bat ears laid back, declaring the area unworthy.

Oliver rolled his eyes. "Fine then; let's go." He turned to head to the barn, but the leash suddenly went taut. Looking over his shoulder, he saw the indecisive dog had decided to do his business after all.

Seriously?

As soon as Creature finished, Oliver yanked on the leash and started to drag the dog back to the barn. Everybody was probably wondering where he was and what was taking so long. Worse yet, he hadn't exactly said where he and Creature were going when they had walked off. They were almost to the barn entrance when they crossed paths with Jason, who was leading a large chestnut gelding. Trailing behind them was another individual, occupied with texting on his cell phone.

"So, Jennifer brought you after all." Jason's face was contorted with irritation. He looked down his perfectly shaped nose at Creature and added, "Are you planning to compete with that fleabag?"

"That joke is as lame as you harassing Jennifer to keep me out of the competition," Oliver retorted.

Jason scoffed. "I'm sure whatever nags you and your cousin have dragged in won't compare to Saint Tobin." He reached up and patted the defined face of his horse. The chestnut snorted, seemingly in agreement. Creature whimpered and darted behind Oliver's legs for protection. "Isn't that right, Phillip?" Jason asked, looking over his shoulder at his friend, who had caught up with them.

Phillip shrugged indifferently and returned to his cell phone. Dark sunglasses covered his eyes, clouding what he thought of Jason's comment. Apparently, judging from his appearance, he wasn't exactly a horsey person; he wore black shorts and a baggy tank top. Curly hair peeked out from underneath the brim of a baseball cap, which was facing backward on his head. A silver hoop earring in his left earlobe completed the grunge look. Whoever Phillip was, he couldn't care less about being there.

Anyhow, Oliver decided he didn't want to stick around any longer, and he started to walk past Jason and his nonchalant sidekick.

"Not so fast." Jason moved and blocked the way.

Great. Now what?

CHAPTER THIRTY-EIGHT

Oliver was missing in action. Again. He had only one job to do, and that was to take Creature out for a quick walk. Thirty minutes later, neither he nor the dog had come back. He didn't answer his phone either when Jennifer texted him. Now that she had finished everything up, it was getting to be time to leave for the hotel. It was necessary to start looking for Oliver. Since Granny and Uncle Stanley had not returned from parking the trailer, the responsibility to find her cousin fell on Jennifer's shoulders.

Where on earth could he be? Jennifer wondered while trying to remember just which direction he had gone.

The Kellert equestrian facility wasn't small; it had a large barn with over a hundred stalls, a small concession stand, and four dressing rooms. Near the barn were five separate riding rings. Three were assigned for warming up, the other two were for the competition courses, and one of those was an indoor arena. Huge spectator stands towered over the outdoor rings, allowing hundreds of people to watch the show. The whole place was specifically designed for competing in show jumping all year round.

Jennifer thought about calling out to Oliver but decided against it. He probably wouldn't hear her. Uncertain where else to start, she took a guess and headed down the barn aisle that led to the back of the property, where there was a large quiet clearing with thick grass and shady trees. A lot of the riders and grooms liked to take their horses there and let them graze since it was secluded and far away from the hubbub of the competition's tense atmosphere. If Oliver had found the clearing by any chance, it was likely that he would've hung around there with Creature.

Jennifer walked all the way to the end of the aisle and made a right. Sure enough, her cousin was standing in the tall doorway with Creature. The concerning part was the fact that they weren't alone. Jason and his friend had somehow managed to find Oliver and were confronting him. No doubt they were in the middle of hurling threats. From past encounters, Jennifer already kind of knew Jason's friend Phillip, who had a bad reputation for being a troublemaker on his own. He wasn't necessarily one to be that interested in Jason's schemes, but for whatever reason, Jason always kept him around. Anyway, instead of only one person after Oliver, they were now two against one.

Her blood now starting to simmer, Jennifer quickened her pace and hurried to intervene before any more damage could be done. Her cousin's nerves were already scrambled enough. Oliver most certainly didn't need Jason *and* Phillip making him even more nervous.

"Hey! What's going on here?" Jennifer marched up, her hot temper rising. Everyone, including Creature and Jason's horse, turned their heads and stared with wide eyes, wondering what wrath they were all about to face.

Be afraid. Be very afraid. "I know what you're up to, Jason. Trying to keep my cousin from competing isn't going to work. Why don't you antagonize someone else for once?"

Oliver and Phillip were speechless, but Jason gave a wry smile, as if he were about to say something. But before he could make a comeback, Jennifer shouldered her way through, knocking his unsuspecting friend to the side like a floppy rag doll. Being the gangly specimen he was, his long arms and legs whirled as Phillip fell flat on his back. Jason's horse startled at the sudden commotion. He threw his head up and began to backpedal away, nearly pulling Jason off his feet. Quick as lightning, Phillip scrambled to get back up. With his sunglasses now twisted and his cap knocked off, his previously cool attitude was ultimately gone as he scooted out of the path of the frightened horse.

"Now looked at what you've caused, you lunatic!" Jason hollered while he tried to regain control over his horse.

"Serves you right," Jennifer snapped back. "Stay away from my cousin!" With that said, she turned to Oliver and said, "C'mon; we're going."

Oliver hesitated, still watching as the upset horse continued to pull away from Jason. Jennifer wasn't willing to wait any longer, though, and grabbed Oliver by the arm, dragging him and Creature along behind her.

It was around seven in the morning when the blaring alarm clock aroused Jennifer. She stirred and stretched her hand out to slap the snooze button but missed. The second attempt to shut up the annoying thing sent it flying off the nightstand, where it continued to screech and vibrate on the floor. Jennifer flipped back the bed covers and managed to snag the alarm clock, silencing it once and for all. Heaving a great sigh, she flopped her head down on the pillow again, wishing that she hadn't been torn out of her peaceful slumber. Uncle Stanley had done her and Oliver the generous favor of going to the barn to feed the horses so they could catch some extra rest at the hotel that morning. But the excitement of competing tomorrow kept Jennifer from falling back asleep. Any hope of closing her eyes was gone when Creature woke up and clambered onto the bed, covering her face with slobbery licks.

Jennifer waved her hands about and fended off the furry terror. Then she turned over on her side and looked across the hotel room, feeling slightly envious of the snoring ball of wadded blankets in the other bed. Oliver could sleep through an earthquake without even knowing. It was so unfair sometimes. Currently cocooned in the blankets that he had wrapped around himself, he was pretty much invisible, apart from one foot hanging over the side of the mattress.

With a resounding bleep, bleep, bleep, the horrid alarm clock suddenly revived itself and made Jennifer and Creature jolt with fright. To add to the racket, Creature started barking in protest. Oliver remained asleep, completely oblivious.

Ugh! This time Jennifer unplugged the cord from the clock to ensure it was good and dead. She wondered if Granny was awake yet. It wouldn't be a surprise if the noise had succeeded in disturbing her sleep. When they came to the hotel last night, they had rented two different rooms; Jennifer and Oliver stayed in one room, while Granny and Uncle Stanley stayed in the adjoining room right next door. As predicted, about fifteen min-utes after the battle with the alarm, Granny was knock-ing on the door and declaring that it was time to get out of bed.

—⊷ ⊶—

The whole morning was a blur for Oliver. It started with his cousin trying to coax him out of bed. Failing to do so, she ripped the blankets away. She gave up tempo-rarily when he tried to seek cover under a pillow that had been left behind. Moments later Jennifer returned with a tub of ice cubes and proceeded to stuff them down the back of Oliver's shirt. Wide awake and wet, he scrambled out of bed and counterattacked Jennifer, beating her with his pillow. Having chased his annoying cousin out of the room, he rushed to get dressed and to catch up with the rest of the group. They all headed over to the waffle house next door for breakfast. After plates of bacon, eggs, and pancakes, heavily drowned in syrup, were scarfed down, Oliver finally found himself straddled on top of Jasper at the horse show.

Today was warm-up day—a last chance to ensure that everything was running smoothly between horse and rider before the actual competition tomorrow. With this fact in mind, everyone was already crowding into the two designated arenas for practice. Preoccupied rid-ers deep in concentration hustled their mounts around, zigzagging in every direction. In the midst of the organized chaos, they managed to practice their flatwork and file over the jumps set out in the middle of the arena.

Jennifer had no trouble navigating among the other riders with Pompeii. Because of the bright-red ribbon tied at the top of his flagging tail to warn others of his kicking habit, the other riders kept their distance. He tossed his head every now and then, flinging gobs of white froth from his mouth into the air. It spattered across the faces of any passing riders and their horses who dared to get close.

With less grace and fluidity than Jennifer, who was experienced with these situations, Oliver grappled with the reins as he guided Jasper through the fray and tried to avoid collisions. Meanwhile, Uncle Stanley's instructions rattled through the radio headsets he and Oliver were wearing.

"Loosen up," Uncle Stanley said from his post at the arena's side. "You're way too tense."

He leaned against the rail and analyzed every movement Oliver made. Uncle Stanley didn't quite fit in with all the other trainers, who were decked out in riding breeches and polo shirts in their barns colors and caps with all the names of the big events stitched on them. Just about every one of them had sunglasses, glinting in the glaring sunlight. Uncle Stanley, on the other hand, was rather sunburned, making him look like a giant red beet dressed in a checkered button-down shirt, faded jeans, and cowboy boots. His matching cowboy hat shaded his face, keeping it from being burned by the sun any more than it already was.

"Watch it!" someone snapped. Startled, Oliver pulled back on Jasper's reins just in time to avoid getting hit by a large chestnut horse. Jason's withering glare appeared and his hand was outstretched, crop waving in the air. He managed to smack it hard across Jasper's nose. It happened so fast that all Oliver could do was hang on as Jasper careened backward. Jason cantered off on his horse, who was lathered in sweat, with bulging veins and eyes rolling wildly. With one last wicked look over his shoulder, Jason disappeared into the moving mass of the other horses and riders.

Uncle Stanley saw the whole incident and immediately went to report it to the seemingly oblivious ring steward who stood nearby, fumbling with a clipboard and a mess of papers. She gave Uncle Stanley a blank stare of cluelessness when he talked to her. Giving up, he came back to the rail.

"Brush it off, son. Forget it happened," Uncle Stanley said. "Focus on your riding instead. Since you are warmed up, let's start going over the crossrails."

CHAPTER THIRTY-NINE

"Does Jason always get away with underhanded things like that?" Oliver asked back at the stables.

Jennifer shrugged and looked up at her cousin, who was standing on a stool in the stall, trying to braid Jasper's scraggly mane for the show. She had been trying to coach him through braiding for over an hour now. So far there was very little progress. Oliver had succeeded in creating three frizzy misshapen balls that were 10 percent hair, 60 percent white yarn, and 30 percent braiding spray. Ironically, Jasper was an easy horse to braid. He didn't even need to be tied, since he was more than content to stand still and munch on hay.

"Most of the time, yeah. Jason's always been the spoiled brat that has the whole system wrapped around every single one of his fingers." Jennifer paused to show Oliver how to secure the braid he was working on. "You gotta thread the needle through the braid, pull the yarn all the way through, and then double back. Think of it as a shish kebab in a way."

"Ow!" Oliver yelped, holding up his hand. "Speaking of fingers, I just skewered my thumb with the needle." Jennifer thought he was exaggerating at first, but sure enough, he had a decent stab wound that was oozing blood. Then came the complaints. "Why are you making me do this? Why can't you help me? You would be so much faster at this."

Jennifer sighed impatiently. "Because you need to learn, that's why."

"Oh, come on. Guys aren't even supposed to braid. This is against nature!"

Oh brother. This is going to take forever. Fortunately, Pompeii's mane was already finished. He looked rather superior in his stall, with a perfect row of tight braids all the way down his muscular neck. Show jumpers didn't always braid their horses' manes, since it wasn't necessarily required at shows, but Jennifer always preferred the tidy look when competing. To her it was like having a trademark that let everyone else know that she cared how she and her horses were presented.

Oliver reluctantly finished sewing in the braid he was working on. "How are they looking?"

"Do you want a sugarcoated answer or the truth?"

"The truth," he said cautiously.

"Those braids look absolutely grotesque." Jennifer glanced down at her wristwatch, and after seeing that it was getting late, she gave in. Oliver was right. It was against nature for him to learn how to braid, at least for today anyway. "Get off the stool," she said. "I'm taking over."

She had never experienced the feeling before, but there was nothing quite as annoying as having to spend her time taking care of someone else's responsibility. Somehow the impish smile on Oliver's face after getting his way didn't really help. He clambered down from the stool and eagerly handed over the braiding equipment. Just as he turned to leave, Jennifer snagged him by the sleeve and stopped him in his tracks. She wasn't about to let him get off that easily.

"Just where do you think you're going in such a hurry?" She smirked as she saw her cousin's temporary sensation of freedom fizzle out like a flash in the pan. She pointed to the nearly empty plastic buckets hanging in the stall and said, "Jasper needs fresh water, so take those buckets with you and fill them. Don't let him die of dehydration."

Jasper nickered as if in agreement and bobbed his golden head, ultimately yanking loose the three snarled braids that had been barely keeping their semi round shape. With a defeated sigh, Oliver grabbed the buckets and left. Jennifer chuckled to herself, enjoying the pleasure of bossing her cousin around. It kind of made up for having to keep him out of trouble. After preparing the braiding equipment and cutting a few sections of yarn for the needle, Jennifer stepped up onto the stool and stared down at Jasper's thin mane. No wonder Oliver was having trouble braiding.

There wasn't really anything left to work with—Jasper had rubbed out most of his mane earlier that summer. He got a bit of a chronic mystery itch every now and then. Not once did he have fungus or rain rot or any other type of skin condition. Last year he had vigorously scratched the top of his tail on everything he could reach, especially wooden things like fences and stall boards. Trees were his favorite. Despite having used every kind of hair-growth-enhancing shampoo, vitamin, and supplement, it had taken a long time for the hair to start growing back. Jasper's tail was still somewhat thin there.

Might as well get started, Jennifer figured. Picking up the bottle of braiding spray, she squirted some on Jasper's sparse mane in hopes of making it sticky enough to stay together when she began braiding.

"I see that your cousin has ditched his work." Jason's annoying voice broke the peaceful quiet. He stepped forward, and his face appeared in front of the cast-iron bars of the stall door. Suddenly, his curly-haired friend Phillip was standing beside him. Double the trouble, they were.

Jennifer scoffed and turned to face them. "Why don't you two go away? I have nothing to say to y'all."

"Oh, but I think you do," Jason replied smugly.

"OK, you got me. I heard about what you did earlier, trying to terrorize my cousin and his horse. He's not even competing against you; *I am.* So why bother him? It'll be a long time before he'll be riding at the level that we're at now."

Phillip finally decided to speak up. "She's got a good point, bro," he said, looking a little uneasy by now, probably remembering yesterday's incident when Jennifer caught Jason harassing her cousin. He started shifting his weight from foot to foot as if he was worried about getting bowled over by Jennifer again. "Maybe we should go."

"Are you kidding? No way, coward." Jason quickly waved him off like a pesky fly. Phillip scowled in return, unamused that he had been belittled. As of that moment, Jennifer wasn't the only one thinking poorly of the braggart.

Not noticing the change in Phillip's demeanor, Jason went on talking. "I'm not stupid. I know that your cousin has talent and his lineage to support him. He's going to be highly sought after by everyone once he finds his niche in the show circuit. It's not a matter of if but when and how soon. It's an unfair advantage, don't you think?"

"It's hardly unfair!" Jennifer cried. She could hardly believe what she was hearing. Was this guy serious? "I think that with your oh-so-brilliant horse, oversize riding facility, and rich parents, you'll be just fine. If I were you, I'd focus on improving my own riding skills rather than waste time trying to give other people grief. So run along, little rich boy; go find a nice money pit to play in. I know how you're deeply attracted to shiny things."

Jason was left speechless, and he opened and closed his mouth, grappling for something equally offending to say as a comeback. His ears turned red, of course. They always did that whenever he got mad because things weren't going his way. Unsurprisingly, he opened his mouth again, as he had found something to say after all. "You're—"

"I said beat it!" Jason stopped midsentence when Jennifer interrupted him. She couldn't stand to listen to another one of his grating remarks. Not now, and not ever. Desperate to get rid of him, she took the bottle of braiding spray she had been holding and squirted the stuff directly in his face. It was perfect timing, as she caught him with his mouth open.

Sputtering and gagging dramatically, the wimp reeled away from the stall door. "My eyes, my eyes!" he wailed as he shoved past Phillip and retreated down the barn aisle, hands clasped over his perfect face as if he had been doused with acid. Oddly enough, Phillip stayed behind, shocked that Jason had received well-deserved payback, which he had managed to avoid for so long.

"Do I need to spray you down as well?" Jennifer aimed the bottle of Quic Braid at Phillip, ready to pull the trigger. To her surprise, he just laughed aloud.

"That was a good shot. Dude really had it coming."

Jennifer dropped her arm in surprise. "I thought you two were best buddies, partners in crime."

"Not really. Jason gets on my nerves on a daily basis," he said, a mischievous smile creeping up and replacing his formerly serious expression. With a wink he added, "That's between us."

Right then they heard Jason shouting from somewhere down the barn aisle. "Phillip, are you going to help me or what? I'm dying here! I need water to rinse my face."

"I guess that's my call. See you around." With a little bow, Phillip turned to go, leaving Jennifer alone with Jasper.

Well, that was interesting.

CHAPTER FORTY

The morning of the show came fast. Since she had one of the early rides, Jennifer was already out in the warm-up arena and waiting for her turn after having walked the course beforehand. She looked sharp in her tailored navy-blue show coat and stark white riding breeches. Her flame-colored hair was neatly contained in a hairnet under her helmet. Pompeii had been groomed to perfection, gleaming under the sun like a combination of melted silver and diamonds. The light filtered right through his thick peppery-gray tail and illuminated the part where it turned white at the bottom. His tack was also quite presentable. Jennifer had put a good amount of effort and time into cleaning up his saddle and bridle, conditioning them until the dark-brown leather was spotless.

Trying to hang on to the leash of a bouncing Creature, Oliver stood by the arena's side with Uncle Stanley and Granny. They closely watched Jennifer work her horse through all the paces and then pop him over a few small jumps. Satisfied that everything was moving smoothly, she took on some of the larger ones. Every once in a while, Uncle Stanley would comment on something over the radio headset and try to help refine things a little.

Jennifer didn't need much help, however. She made jumping look effortless when she directed Pompeii at a vertical that was set at a meter twenty. Practice jumps were usually set at the height of the jump course in the show arena. Jennifer and Pompeii approached the vertical at a steady pace, and when Pompeii raised his head eagerly and began to surge forward, Jennifer calmly eased him back until they found the right distance for takeoff. Pompeii launched himself upward like a rocket, with his knees tucked tight, and he cleared the vertical with feet to spare.

It was exhilarating to watch Pompeii jumping; the horse lifted his massive body into the air with ease. His large front hooves would make contact with the ground, and his thin legs somehow absorbed the hard impact each time they landed. Sand that was slightly damp from the morning dew spattered upward onto Pompeii's broad chest from the detonation of his feet pummeling the ground while he cantered on to the next jump.

Oliver was so engrossed that he didn't notice anyone talking to him until Uncle Stanley reached over and tapped his shoulder. He startled like he always did when being ripped out of a daydream, his heart thudding after watching Jennifer and Pompeii. Would that be him one day?

Uncle Stanley looked serious and focused, but he had a small twinkle in eyes. "This afternoon when you ride, you'll basically be doing the same thing Jennifer is now. You'll warm up, go over some jumps, and then go in the show ring when they call you. The only difference is that the jumps will be smaller."

"OK," Oliver responded, but he wasn't listening. Jennifer had already grilled him about what they would be doing in the show. She was practically a walking encyclopedia about horses and anything that involved them. Every opportunity she had, she would stuff information into him, whether he wanted to learn or not, and if there was something he needed to know, she ensured that he learned whatever it was. Nevertheless, Uncle Stanley continued to drone on, explaining all the steps of what to do.

"Good boy!" Jennifer slowed Pompeii down and patted him on the neck. They had both broken a sweat from the fast-paced workout. "How much time do I have before I go in?" she asked as they ambled over to the arena's side. Creature got excited and started pulling toward her, nearly yanking Oliver off his feet again. He jerked hard on the leash to get the dog to behave, but Creature didn't even care. Instead he just flopped around like a captive fish on the end of a line.

"Soon," Uncle Stanley said. He looked down at his wrist and checked his watch. "There's one rider about to go, and then you'll be next."

Jennifer and Pompeii didn't have to wait long. In a matter of five minutes, the ring steward was already calling out for the next rider to come in. "Number one hundred and twenty, you're up!" she announced loudly.

"It's time to go, Oliver," Granny said excitedly. "Let's go find our seats."

She ushered him toward the spectator stands, while Uncle Stanley walked with Jennifer to the gate. Granny was dressed up today in a flowery sundress and a floppy straw hat. Bright-red lipstick and a pound of heavily applied foundation, eyeshadow, and mascara made her look a few years younger. In one hand, she clung onto an antique device that appeared to be a 1970s Polaroid camera. How it still functioned was a mystery. Oliver checked for his cell phone and was pleased to feel it in his pants pocket. It couldn't hurt take some pictures as well. Jennifer would probably appreciate some digital pictures in color for once.

Granny found a row of seats with the best view. They were angled toward the side of the arena, so they could see the whole jump course. As soon as she sat down, she immediately began inspecting her artifact of a camera. The people sitting behind Granny weren't pleased about their view being blocked by her large hat. Of course she was oblivious to their discontent; she was too busy paying attention to Jennifer as she entered the arena.

"Oh, here she comes!" Granny held up her camera and got ready to start snapping photos. Somewhat discreetly, Oliver did the same with his cell phone. Situated between his legs, Creature began to whine fretfully. The dimwitted dog never could figure out where Jennifer had disappeared to.

The air was thick with suspense, which was sort of electrifying and scary at the same time to watch, mainly because it was exactly how it would go when it was Oliver's turn to ride. The bustling crowd hushed as Jennifer halted her jiggling horse in front of the judges and saluted. They rang the bell, signaling for her to start. She pushed her horse into a rhythmic canter and rode through the markers. The time, which was displayed on a big screen near the arena, started counting down the seconds. The goal was to ride the fastest with the fewest faults. It was a tricky feat, considering how easy it was to knock down rails. Knocking over jumps added time faults.

There were thirteen jumps in the course, all of which were set up at different angles and distances. The first combination was two verticals about five strides apart. Pompeii took on both of them with a fervor that Jennifer could barely contain. With his head held high and his tail flagging, he fought the bit vigorously as he tore around the course, throwing himself over every obstacle Jennifer pointed him at. His habit of taking off a little too early before jumping had the audience on edge. When it appeared that he was going to drag the rail down with his hind legs, he would kick them up at the last second and clear it. Then the audience would gasp at the hair-raising sharp turns that Pompeii would take, leaning so far toward the ground that he could have fallen onto his side.

At one minute fifty seconds, Jennifer and her gray gelding cleared the last jump and ripped through the finish line. In their chaotic fashion, they had made a clear round. The audience cheered and clapped. Granny shocked Oliver by standing up and applauding more loudly than anyone else. While the announcer tried to talk over the audience, Jennifer showered Pompeii with praise and headed out of the gate to where Uncle Stanley waited with a big grin on his sunburned face. Granny jumped up and hurtled down the stairs of the spectator stand as fast as a woman her age could go. Oliver trailed behind her, a little anxious that she was going to trip and plummet headfirst all the way to the bottom. But with Creature pulling on the leash and hopping two steps at a time, Oliver was pretty sure that if anyone fell, it would be him.

They caught up with Jennifer and Uncle Stanley at the barn. Jennifer had already dismounted and was attempting to hug Pompeii while he wiped his big sweaty face on her show coat. He left behind a generous smear of slobber stained pink from the red-and-white-striped peppermints she had fed him. She just laughed in good humor and hugged the obnoxious monster again. Uncle Stanley patted Pompeii on the shoulder and congratulated Jennifer on her good ride. Granny and Oliver stood back, keeping a safe distance. Neither of them wanted frothy horse slobber smeared on their clothes, although Creature kept trying to pull Oliver's arm off in his efforts to get to Jennifer. Eventually Jennifer led Pompeii away to get him untacked and hosed down. They were certainly a unique duo.

Jennifer placed first in her class, while Jason landed a shocking fifth place after knocking down rails and having a refusal. Something like that was unheard of for him, according to Jennifer. With the help of good trainers, indispensable horses, and a luxurious riding facility at his fingertips, he scored in the top three at every competition. There had been no exceptions. That is, until now.

━◦+ +◦━

Sweaty and tired from her ride, Jennifer slouched on top of a tack trunk in front of Pompeii's stall. As she sat there, she replayed the course in her mind, relishing her first-place finish. She couldn't help but also wonder about Jason having finished in fifth place. Did it have anything to do with her squirting the braiding spray in his eyes? One could only guess.

Either way, at the moment the most she could think about was getting back to the hotel later and cooling off under the air conditioner. The sun was playing its wicked game of scorching the air and creating an outdoor sauna. It was so hot that it was almost suffocating. She couldn't wait for autumn to go into full swing. It was her favorite season because it was neither too hot nor too cold. Having cool rain every once in a while was nice as well.

But the middle of autumn hadn't entirely arrived yet, and it was still miserably hot. The sun had to be laughing at all this, no doubt. Jennifer sighed and opened a bottle of Gatorade that Uncle Stanley had handed her earlier before he'd left with Granny to double-check the ride times. She gulped down the cold, refreshing liquid, grateful for some relief from the sweaty state she was in. There was a long pitiful whine from by her feet. Jennifer looked down and laughed at her frazzled dog, who was convinced that the Gatorade was something she ought to share.

"Sorry, bud, but you can't have it. Drink your water instead." Jennifer pushed a Styrofoam cup of water toward Creature that she had tried to offer to him a few minutes ago. He sniffed it in distaste and then turned it over, spilling the water across the cement floor of the barn. Obviously he still didn't want it.

"Hey, can you help me?" Oliver suddenly grumbled from inside Jasper's stall. He had been getting his horse cleaned up and the tack set out for his ride. Jennifer realized that it was forty minutes before Oliver needed to mount, and he still had to get his show clothes on. What was taking so long? It wasn't that big of a deal to brush a horse down. On the other hand, the poop stains that Jasper liked to smear into his golden coat when he rolled were rather hard to remove.

"Jennifer, are you there?" Oliver called once more. "Jasper's rubbed out his braids again!"

Ugh, again? This time, she was the one to grumble. Jasper was almost impossible to maintain during a show. He had destroyed just about every one of his braids last night, and Jennifer had to help Oliver fix them all this morning. Now here they were, having to go through the same ordeal just four hours later. "Hang on; I'm coming," Jennifer said.

Luckily it did not take long to fix the braids. Jasper had only succeeded in rubbing out a couple of them. The rest looked a little gnarly, but there wasn't enough time to be finicky about them. All Jennifer could do was take scissors and snip away the most gruesome-looking strands of hair that protruded from each braid. The forelock was an entirely different case. There was barely any hair left after Jasper had ripped out the braid. As a last-ditch effort to cover it, Jennifer borrowed Pompeii's stark-red ear net and put it on Jasper when they tacked him up.

"Go get changed," Jennifer said, sending her cousin out of the stall so he wouldn't hover. He wasn't that useful anyhow with his show nerves setting in. "I'll have Jasper ready to go when you come back."

"OK…" Oliver hesitated, then asked, "Are you sure?"

"Yes," she reassured him. "Now go on; get!"

Being obedient, Oliver took off for the dressing room. The sight of him running down the barn aisle like a schoolkid who was late for class, with his white breeches and his show coat folded over his arm, made Jennifer smile.

Her cousin was no longer the introverted stranger who she had seen that first day, sitting on the living-room couch and closed off from the world. He had changed completely. Seven months ago, Jennifer never would've believed that she would have someone like him shoved into her life and turning it upside down. Now she couldn't imagine not having him around—driving her crazy, making her angry, inspiring her to laugh, creating new memories, and being someone who she would care about forever. Better yet, he was a friend to share her passion for horses with. It was as if his being in her life was meant to be. Sometimes even the worst things imaginable could turn out to be miracles. Nightmares turned into desired dreams.

CHAPTER FORTY-ONE

I t was a struggle to change into the tight riding breeches and shirt while being sticky with sweat, but Oliver managed to do it quickly. The air conditioner kept the dressing room at a comfortable temperature, just chilly enough to combat the hot weather outside. For a brief second, he was tempted to hide inside here rather than face having to ride. So many thoughts flashed through his mind as he imagined all the scenarios that could play out. What if he did badly? What if he disappointed everyone? Mainly he didn't want to fail at this competition, especially not after working so hard to get to the point he was at.

Oliver shook his head in an attempt to fling away the disturbing vision of messing up. Anyhow, everyone would most certainly ring his neck if he did decide to hide in the dressing room. Backing out now wasn't an option. After checking himself in the mirror and ensuring that everything was straight, Oliver picked up his show coat and shrugged it on. Freshly dry-cleaned and recently tailored, it fit snugly around his body. The silver buttons shined and glistened from being polished. Even the red collar had been carefully ironed so the edges laid just so across the shoulders.

The only thing that was awry, though, was the peculiar bulge in the left pocket. Oliver attempted to flatten it but to no avail. Curiosity growing, he reached inside the pocket and felt something. He wrapped his hand around it and came back out with an old crumpled envelope.

Huh, what's this? he wondered, turning it over and examining the off-white paper that was tattered and bent from when the coat had been cleaned and ironed. Interestingly, the envelope was still sealed shut after ages of being in the pocket. Whoever had slipped it in there had addressed it to his father, Daniel, but he'd never found it—or at least he had never opened it. Where did it come from? Oliver opened the tattered envelope and read the letter that was in slightly better condition.

Dear son,

    I am not very good with words or at conversing with others. Sometimes you have the same issue. So I have taken the alternative to voicing my thoughts and decided to put them on paper instead.

I know you may feel like there is a lot of pressure for you to win the USEF National Show tomorrow. But understand that whatever takes place, I will always be proud of you. If you lose, I won't even mention a word about the competition. It'll be as if it had never happened. I assure you that we won't lose the farm though. One way or another, we will find a way to work through this tough period.

Remember what I have always told you: keep strong, not only physically but mentally.

—Your father, Louis Murray

Feeling nostalgic, Oliver held on to the old letter for a moment, realizing that it had been written by none other than Granddad. Oliver's father must not have known that the letter was stowed away in the coat pocket. Considering that their relationship had been strained to begin with, things really must have started falling apart when Granddad had thought that his son had read the letter but never bothered to acknowledge it.

It was remarkable how a single letter could have the power to cause a small tear in something barely threaded together. Then that tear, although small at first, gradually got bigger and bigger until it was irreparable.

The way that things had turned out for the family was unfortunate, but it had set a good example. Oliver knew one thing for sure: he wasn't going to make the same mistakes and abuse his second chance at having a family after already losing one. Every moment with them counted, no matter how small and simple it might seem.

Jennifer and Granny were the first ones to see Oliver dressed up in his show clothes when he returned from the dressing room. They fussed over him, complimenting his tidied appearance and admiring how handsome he looked in his show coat. With a whimsical smile stretching from ear to ear, Granny helped straighten his tie so it would be perfect.

"You look just like your father, you know." Granny chuckled softly. "Even down to your wild hair." She took her hand and attempted to brush Oliver's hair back, but his lion's mane just wasn't meant to be tamed. The heat and humidity definitely didn't do it any favors. His hair was battling a major case of frizz. Coming to the rescue, Jennifer stepped up and crammed a helmet over his head, stating that it would help in the meantime, but he had to get mounted now.

Right on cue, Uncle Stanley came down the barn aisle with Jasper, who was glistening brighter than a polished bar of gold. He looked Oliver up and down and gave a quiet nod of approval. "Let's go, son," he said, handing off the horse.

"Thanks." Oliver took the reins and led Jasper out of the barn, his posse following closely behind. He spotted a mounting block near the warm-up arena and climbed aboard the horse. It felt weird to suddenly be high up and looking down on everyone. They were all so excited. Eager smiles stretched across each face. Granny snapped a quick photo with her ancient camera to capture the moment. It would match perfectly with the rest of her old photo collection that she had around the house—special memories of her life that she had frozen in place.

Oliver remembered the letter he had found. "Wait, I have something to show you." He dug the letter out of his pocket and held it out for Granny. Bemused, she took it and analyzed it. Her expression morphed into amazement when she saw that it was from her departed husband.

"Oh my, what's this?" she said aloud as she read the letter. Uncle Stanley and Jennifer got curious and sidled up next to her to see.

"It was in my pocket. Granddad must've left it for my dad to find, but I don't think he ever found it," Oliver explained.

"So they didn't truly hate each other after all," Granny said in realization. She placed a hand on her heart, overcome with newfound relief. "It was all a misunderstanding." Her eyes got misty. So did Uncle Stanley's, shockingly enough. Somehow knowing that

Grandfather Louis hadn't blamed his son was very comforting to the whole family in that instant.

As touching as this was, time was ebbing away, and Oliver had to get to the arena if he was going to compete. The warm-up flew by in what seemed like a few seconds. But it went fairly well, proving to everyone that Oliver and Jasper were ready to take on the real action. Thankfully the nerves that had made his stomach flutter that morning had ceased. There was nothing to worry about. As Uncle Stanley had said, the competition was all going to be a piece of cake. Oliver had already walked the course and memorized it prior to riding. The jumps were all set to ninety centimeters, lower than what he had been jumping back home. Also Jasper was more than experienced from years of showing. He would have no trouble negotiating the course, as long as Oliver used a lot of leg and let him do his job. At least that was what Jennifer claimed anyway.

Before Oliver knew it, his number was being called. He didn't hear the ring steward shouting it out for a third time. It was Uncle Stanley who alerted him by waving his arms around and motioning toward the gate. He would have used the radio to talk to Oliver, but it was against the rules to wear communication devices in the competition arena.

"Come on; it's time to go in!" Uncle Stanley said breathlessly. He did one last check of Jasper's tack, making sure that everything was in order. Granny was already making a beeline for seats in the spectator stands with Creature. The red dog served as a motor, practically dragging her up the steps while she grasped the opposite end of the worn-out leash. It was a miracle that she didn't get pulled off her feet.

Jennifer stayed behind momentarily. She crossed over and put her face next to Jasper's ear and whispered something. Oliver watched, perplexed, as she took hold of the horse's bridle and stared into his deep-brown eyes expectantly, as if she was searching for an indication that he understood whatever she had told him. The horse let out a snort to get rid of a fly that had landed on his nose. It was good enough for Jennifer. She looked up at Oliver and smiled with satisfaction.

"What did you tell him?" he asked, trying not to laugh.

She had that mischievous look again. "He'll take good care of you. Just hang on and enjoy the ride." Jennifer gave Oliver a reassuring pat on the leg before taking off to catch up with Granny.

Uncle Stanley sent Oliver through the gate into the arena. He gave a thumbs-up and said, "You've got this. Go knock their socks off."

As he had practiced before, Oliver went toward the judges' stand and halted Jasper in front of the critical-looking people inside. He tipped his head to let them know he was ready. The bell rang in response. It was sort of a soft ting that quickly dissipated in the air. Looking back over his shoulder, he saw Uncle Stanley waving his hand and signaling that it was OK to go. They had planned this beforehand in case Oliver did not hear the bell.

Everything seemed awfully quiet all at once. The only thing that Oliver could hear was his own heart thudding against his ribs. Despite having dozens of people in the stands watching with anticipation, he felt alone. The vast size of the arena and the clear blue sky overhead threatened to swallow him like a bug. Jasper moved underneath Oliver, reminding him that he wasn't entirely by himself.

Well, this is it. Just you and me, buddy, Oliver thought.

Snapping out of his momentary stupor, Oliver clasped his legs around Jasper and urged him through the starting line. The first jump was foreboding to a horse. Its rails were striped bright blue and white, and a row of potted flowers were lined up at the bottom. Jasper didn't balk whatsoever at the jump. He pricked his ears and lunged for it. Jennifer was not kidding about him knowing how to tackle a course.

Oliver already had his head turned and was looking for the second jump when they landed. Jasper sensed the shift of weight in the stirrups and turned on a dime, saving precious seconds. The next jump came up fast. It was set up a sharp angle, and Oliver had to sit back and coax the palomino back a little so they would not overshoot it. Jasper immediately slowed just enough and adjusted his stride, taking off right on the mark. Once they got into their rhythm, the rest of the jumps were pretty easy and straightforward. Jasper attacked them all like an old pro. Not a single rail was dropped as he tucked up his legs. His neck and withers lifted up into an arc as he left the ground and soared over each jump.

There was just one last jump to tackle—the oxer. Of course the hardest one was saved for the end. It was painted black and red, with matching flowers gathered around the large jump stands that fanned out to the sides. Most of the riders that had gone before Oliver and Jasper had wound up either knocking down the rails or having their horses refuse to jump altogether. Oliver readied Jasper for the intimidating oxer and counted the strides.

One...two...three...

On the third stride, Jasper's gathered himself and pushed off the ground with his powerful hind legs. He launched into the air, bringing his legs up underneath him to clear the rails. Oliver stretched his hands over the crest of the horse's neck, all the while holding his breath as they seemed to hang in the air for a moment. It was such a beautiful feeling—the suspense—waiting to see if they would make it or not.

Then they came back down to earth and landed. The impact of Jasper's solid hooves slamming against the ground vibrated all the way up his legs and through Oliver's body. His heart was in his throat now from the adrenaline pumping in his bloodstream. They had made it.

The announcer's voice boomed over the speaker when they raced through the finish line. "That's a clear round of one minute forty-five seconds for Oliver Murray and his mount, Jasper's Sunrise!" The audience began to applaud afterward.

Oliver slowed Jasper down to a trot and patted him on the neck. "Good boy!"

Uncle Stanley greeted them at the arena gate and shared his congratulations. "Great job out there," he said with a beaming smile, giving Oliver's back one of his whopping pats. "You're the last rider in your class, and you placed second with your time! Look at the board."

Oliver looked up at the electronic screen that stood over the arena, displaying the times of the riders who had competed. He could hardly believe it. Sure enough, he was firmly in second place. Not bad for a first show. He'd actually done better than he had hoped for. He and Uncle Stanley headed back to the barn so they could cool Jasper off. Just as Oliver was about to dismount, he spotted Jennifer running up, with Granny and Creature following a few feet behind her.

Fueled by pure ecstasy and the undying excitement of riding in his first competition, Oliver sailed out of the saddle and met up with Jennifer. She screeched with surprise as he trapped her in a bear hug and twirled, lifting her off the ground just enough for her feet to dangle. Granny and Uncle Stanley started laughing, and Jasper flicked his ears at the commotion everyone was making. With an inquisitive snort, the horse shoved his nose between Jennifer and Oliver, demanding the treat they owed him.

"Jasper!" Jennifer exclaimed. "You little pig." She relented and gave him a few sticky peppermints that Pompeii hadn't scarfed down yet.

Things aren't so bad after all, Oliver realized when he observed the smiling faces of his family surrounding him. He had lost his past, but there was still a future to cultivate. More importantly, he wasn't alone; he had a new family who loved him all the same.

THE END

ABOUT THE AUTHOR

 Nicole Rothell lived her childhood in South Africa, Mexico, Brazil, and Texas. From an early age, animals were a part of her life. Always an avid horse lover, Nicole competed in eventing and dressage from the age of seven. The same love of horses led her to choose a future in equestrian sports. Nicole believes that each and every horse she has ridden over the years has taught her valuable lessons about how to overcome all challenges and adversities.

To learn more about Nicole Rothell visit her website at: Nicolerothell.com

www.ingramcontent.com/pod-product-compliance
Lightning Source LLC
Chambersburg PA
CBHW050013180626
46810CB00002B/397